Mistaken Marquess

A Regency romance

by

Susan Leona Fisher

Regency Imposter Series, Book 2

We have all a better guide in ourselves, if we would attend to it, than any other person can be.

Mansfield Park, by Jane Austen

Cover

Regency interior (copyright, the author)

Dedication

In tribute to portrait artists of long ago, who gave us such skilful images of historical figures in pre-photographic times.

Published by Susan Leona Fisher, 2022

Acknowledgments

My thanks as ever to the British Library for its increasingly expanding digital archive, making so many scanned-in books and documents available on-line, and also for their British Newspaper Archive, the source of much helpful contemporary detail.

About the story

Lady Cordelia Penshurst, at twenty-four, is little changed from the timid, anxious child who first came to live in her grandfather's house in Berkeley Square, under the chaperonage of Lady Millicent Dunwoody. She is obedient and unquestioning, even concerning her interminable betrothal to the elusive Marquess of Dartington, whom she's not seen for eight years and to whom her only link is a portrait by a renowned artist, which looks quite unlike the man she remembers. When a financial crisis overtakes the household, they decide to raise funds by selling the painting, doubting they'll ever see him again.

Captain Henry Stanhope, on leave from the Peninsular Wars while his ship undergoes repairs, arrives in London intending to enjoy the summer social season. He is quite surprised to discover that a rumour is soon spreading around the *haut ton* that he is the missing Marquess of Dartington. When he views the portrait he realises why, although at twenty-eight he is far too young for the part. In the course of solving the mystery, he learns more about Cordelia's circumstances and when Lady Millicent falls seriously ill, it is Henry who encourages Cordelia to face up to her responsibilities and take some control of her life instead of letting everyone else run it for her.

1: Short of funds

Friday 15th May 1812, Berkeley Square

A single young lady, known to command a generous dowry, is an irresistible temptation to a single gentleman of any age. Whatever scandal surrounds her origins, however unprepossessing her appearance—these failings will readily be overlooked, if she is perceived as a source of untold wealth. This was the philosophy in which Lady Cordelia Penshurst had been reared. Now, as she gazed at her twenty-four-year-old self in the substantial gilt-framed mirror that filled the wall above the drawing room fireplace, she wondered, not for the first time, whether lucre was all that was needed.

Why else had she waited these past eight years for her supposed betrothed to return and duly speak the words that would make them man and wife? Grandpapa, while there was yet breath in his body, had persisted in the line that the enterprising marquess was busy making his fortune in the Americas and would return a rich man and give her a fine life. But Grandpapa had breathed his last five years ago and, with every passing year since, her hope that the Marquess of Dartington would appear on his dashing white charger and carry her off to a life of luxury continued to fade until she truly believed him to be dead also.

Besides his non-appearance, what of the rumoured dowry? Cordelia sometimes wondered if her grandfather might have naïvely given it to the man in advance, for she'd heard nothing further about it. As for the other attributes required to succeed in the marriage market, words such as accomplished, beautiful, intelligent and lively flashed through her mind. She'd certainly possessed none of these qualities when, as a slightly plump and extremely gauche sixteen-year-old, she had agreed to Grandpapa's arrangement, encouraged by his friend, the Lady Millicent Dunwoody. Lady Millicent had resided in his town house for years and had become Cordelia's chaperone, from that sad day, at the age of five, when she had come to live with them. Lady Millicent was wont to remind her at every opportunity that she'd since developed none of those qualities expected by society—how could she when they couldn't afford the expense of a good governess and a dance tutor? They would simply have to remain grateful to her late grandfather for arranging her betrothal to such a worthy man. She had only to be patient until his return.

Staring at her reflection now, Cordelia decided it must be that she was not pretty enough. Her figure was perhaps pleasing enough, now neat and trim with womanly curves, but without being voluptuous. Examining her face, she was not sure anyone could really call it ugly. It was heart-shaped, as her mother's had been, although she had no clear memory of her. There was a miniature in what had been her grandfather's study which proved it, along with evidence of the same blonde hair. Cordelia's thick tresses were currently tamed to neatness in a single plait, which was coiled about the top of her head, but her rebellious locks always allowed a few rogue curls to escape. Her eyes were not the same blue as her mother's but more of a grey shade. Still, she had a mouth where a mouth should be and likewise a nose, which was reasonably straight, unlike the somewhat hooked version sported by Lady Millicent. Cordelia wondered if that was what had attracted the lady to keep a South American parrot as a pet, for *Scarlet*, as she called the atrocious thing, had a similar hooked beak.

The evidence of her own eyes told Cordelia that she really did not look too awful. But, according to Lady Millicent, she could never be called pretty while she continued to wear that frown upon her face. The small crease between her brows, resembling an upside-down V, was ever there to some degree, even when she felt relatively benign towards life, which she did when she escaped this rather mean terraced house on the north side of Berkeley Square and ambled alone amongst the shrubs and flowers of the huge railed garden that filled the square. Her lack of fashionable beauty was further emphasised by the clothes she wore. Today, Cordelia had on a walking outfit that had been the height of fashion some four or five years ago. It was one of her smartest assemblages, but she knew enough of the modern trends to suspect she'd quite likely receive some thinly-veiled sniggers from fashion-conscious females, when she accompanied Lady Millicent to Bond Street this morning.

Everything about her dress that had once made it the height of popularity, now screamed how out-of-date it was. The neck was too high, the sleeves too tight and long and the predominantly white cambric, which then had been thought light and chaste, was now deemed too insipid. And who these days wore a straw hat ornamented with spring flowers, or had a dress that was laced up behind and had frogs embroidered around the border?

Cordelia's self-condemnation was interrupted by the click of the door being opened by one of the maids and Lady Millicent made her cumbersome entry. She did not walk so well these days.

"Ah…here you are, Cordelia. I need to speak with you, she said, in her usual superior and strident tone, for she had also become somewhat hard of hearing and was unaware how loudly she spoke. That could be most embarrassing on social occasions when the old lady's little confidential asides—well, in all honesty, titbits of gossip—were pronounced, like a town crier, for all to hear. How fortunate they received so few invitations. Cordelia tried not to raise her own voice, when speaking to Lady Millicent. Instead, she had developed the habit of speaking slowly and enunciating the consonants at the start and end of each word. She suspected others hearing it might think she was talking to a backward child!

"Yes, Lady M. I'm ready to go. Do I require a pelisse, do you think?" She took in her ladyship's outfit—a mauve gown in a heavy brocade, with a black mantle around her shoulders and a turban-style headdress in black felt, missing its veil. The absent veil was, of course, the purpose of their outing today, for the ancient piece of lace had developed a hole too big to be mended. Cordelia thought the awful parrot must be the guilty party, but nothing had been said. It hardly needed to be, for why else had the squawking creature's cage been removed from her ladyship's bedchamber and placed here in the corner of the drawing room? That had been its original abode, until banished upstairs after calling the visiting rector a *pretty boy*. These days there were too few visitors for it to matter.

"It would be advisable, my dear," her ladyship said, in answer to Cordelia's question. "Adèle tells me there is a slight breeze—leastways I believe that is what she meant by *une petite brise*. It's so many years since I did the grand tour."

It was amazing to recall that the Frenchwoman had been employed as Lady Millicent's personal maid since before Cordelia had come to live here—more than twenty years at least—yet still they appeared to have difficulty communicating with each other! *Scarlet*, on the other hand, who'd resided here about the same length of time, Cordelia suspected might be bi-lingual, although his vocabulary was somewhat limited, as well as superbly wicked. She had a quiet smile to herself at the thought, as she glanced across at the cage. It was currently covered over, which gave them respite from its usual invectives.

The maid Adèle was to accompany them to the modiste's shop in Bond Street, since they no longer employed a footman to fulfil escort duties for such an outing. Besides, her French was occasionally of use when discussing the more technical points of mantua-making with the French seamstress. Cordelia found it ironic that, while Great Britain might be at war with France, British society still valued French maids and French fashions.

"You wanted a word?" Cordelia reminded the elderly lady. She did tend to forget things these days.

"Did I? Oh, so I did. Let us sit." Lady Millicent sank onto the sofa to one side of the fireplace, rested her stick against the arm and patted the cushion beside her.

Cordelia dutifully did as she was told—when did she not? Lady Millicent then did a most unusual thing. She clasped Cordelia's nearest hand between both her own hands. For a moment, Cordelia wondered if the old lady was inspecting Cordelia's fingernails, for she was staring unblinking at the hand she held.

"My dear…I…er…I need to speak about some serious matters."

Cordelia felt those frown creases between her brows deepen. "Oh?"

Lady Millicent inhaled a deep breath and then let it slowly out. "Dear me, I should probably have informed you sooner."

"Are you ill, my lady?" Cordelia asked, all concern.

"No, nothing like that...although I do feel a little sick at the thought of the business. No, my dear, it concerns money."

"I see," Cordelia murmured, half to herself. She was not surprised, for had she not noticed the various economies the household had been making of late? Cook had cut down on groceries and these days they ate more vegetables than meat. What meat they had tended to be the cheaper cuts. Throughout last winter, they had eaten at three and grown accustomed to retire early, avoiding the lighting of the drawing room fire for the evening and saving on lamp oil and candles. It had been some time since Cordelia had enjoyed the luxury of a fire in her own chamber in the winter. It did not bother her, she had simply arranged for an additional quilt. Then, of course, the small chaise, together with the pony which pulled it, had been sold last year and the stableman, who was also the driver, had been let go. Neither had she nor Lady Millicent given custom to their regular dressmaker lately, save in the purchase of the odd piece of lace or ribbon.

One economy they had not taken was any thought of cancelling their daily newspaper delivery. For Lady Millicent, the *Morning Post* was about the only glimpse into high society she enjoyed these days and, at sixpence an issue, Cordelia supposed it a good deal cheaper than meeting the expense of fashionable outfits and transport to attend social events in person. As for herself, Cordelia liked to keep up with political news and progress with the Peninsular War. Leastways, that was what she persuaded herself. She could not help spotting the odd paragraph about South America, but never saw the Marquess of Dartington mentioned.

Lady Millicent's expression was still contorted with anxiety and she seemed to be struggling to explain further. Cordelia waited quietly, tipping her head on one side in a question to invite the lady to continue. At last, she did so.

"Yes...money. The fact is, Cordelia, we have none. Your grandfather, bless him, left us well provided for, as I thought, but it appears we've been drawing on the pot of money he left, so to speak, rather than a using a regular sum of income from investments. There *are* no investments. And quite soon there will be not a penny left in the pot."

"What does grandfather's attorney have to say about it? Have you spoken with him?" Cordelia knew little about money matters, for did not the men see to all that, with a legal man to help them?

Lady Millicent's lined face screwed up into a frown a lot more expressive than the one she regularly complained about on Cordelia's face. "Useless man! Dear Charles has been dead what...five years at least. Mr Steadfast must have been aware of our precarious situation back then, but said not a word. We might have instituted economies sooner."

Cordelia tried to think it through. "But surely our right to live in this house was laid down in Grandpapa's will?"

"Indeed it was, an arrangement in place until your marriage. But we must still meet the running costs and pay the servants." Lady Millicent dragged her faded blue eyes from focusing on Cordelia's hand held in hers to look into Cordelia's own questioning ones. "I doubt he anticipated such a long period of betrothal."

"Because he always thought the Marquess would turn up—*on the next ship*, as he always put it—but he hasn't and, quite honestly Lady M, I'm not sure he ever will." It was the first occasion on which Cordelia had actually expressed this thought aloud, although she'd considered it privately many times. She felt no hopeless sorrow at expressing this probable truth. If anything, it gave her a sense of relief. There was an unreality about being betrothed so long ago to a man whom she really knew not at all. She could barely picture him in her mind, although Grandpapa had made sure to have him sit for his portrait before he departed on his travels. No guesses as to who had paid for that! It was kept in his study, a room she hardly ever entered. She certainly did not stand and gaze at it with any sense of longing, nor an iota of regret that he'd not returned to wed her.

Strangely, it was that portrait Lady Millicent now mentioned. She let go Cordelia's hand, pushed herself up from the sofa and took hold of her stick. "I have an idea that may help the situation. It concerns the Marquess's picture. Come."

To reach Grandpapa's study they only had to cross the hall and enter the small room that had served as his office and his library. It was rarely used these days and Cordelia sniffed at the musty aroma and the enduring hint of stale tobacco, as they entered. The surface of the old desk was dulled by a film of dust, as were the two decanters that sat upon it, except for several finger marks visible on the glass surface. Lady M was losing her grip on the servants, as well as everything else.

The walls were mostly lined with book shelves, leaving little free wall space on which to hang pictures. The collection of family miniatures, including her mother's, filled a small section on one side of the door, while on the other side was displayed a head and shoulders picture of the Marquess of Dartington. It was so positioned that it was the last object one focused on before leaving the room. No doubt her grandfather had gazed upon it a lot more frequently than had Cordelia. She wondered what thoughts had gone through his head when he did so. Did he regret the failed arrangement he had made with the man?

They both stood before the picture and studied it in silence for a moment or two.

"Handsome man," Lady Millicent commented.

"Ooo…certainly this version makes him look so." It had been some time since she'd entered this room and viewed the image and a full eight years since she'd seen the original. "I rather think the artist has been generous in his portrayal."

Lady Millicent stepped closer and peered at the picture. It was not only her hearing that was deteriorating. "What do you mean?"

"Well, I know I only met the man twice and spent little enough time in his company, but as I recall, his hairline was noticeably receding. He was thirty-two, after all. Also, his sideburns were tinged with grey. I remember thinking at the time, my goodness, this fellow is twice my age and doesn't he look it!"

Lady Millicent gave her a quick glance—possibly a slight pang of guilt—before turning her attention back to the portrait. "Yes, I see. Here he has a very healthy head of dark brown hair and those dark brows above warm brown eyes."

Cordelia stepped closer and rested her hands on her hips. "I don't know who the artist was, but he certainly took liberties with the truth. I remember the Marquess as having somewhat wishy-washy hazel eyes and they were a lot closer together than portrayed here—smaller too. Also, his nose is wrong. It wasn't straight like this but had a distinct bony lump in the middle and came to an odd little point at the end that was all pink and shiny. And his mouth turned down a noticeable amount on one side. It wasn't straight like this, nor so full-lipped. He's got the slight dimple in the chin right, though, but the shape's wrong. As I recall, the marquess had a more pointed chin, slightly receding, not broad and strong like this one."

"It's so hard to remember," Lady Millicent said. "Can you read the artist's signature, Cordelia? In the bottom right-hand corner there?"

Cordelia stepped closer. "*J*, I think, then *H…o…p…p*—"

"Hoppner!" Lady Millicent exclaimed. "John Hoppner. I thought so. He was a member of the Royal Academy and official painter to the Prince Regent."

"Was?"

"He died, something over a year ago, I believe. It's rather odd, if, as you suggest, this is so unlike the man. Mr Hoppner was renowned as the truthful painter."

"Well, Grandpapa was paying for it. Do you think he asked the artist to…make some adjustments?"

"Hm…you may be right. He possibly wanted you to remember him in a kinder light."

"A more handsome one, you mean. I wonder if he paid extra for the privilege. If so, he was wasting his money. The image of the first time I met him stayed with me. I thought him not handsome at all, nor a particularly fine figure. His belly protruded somewhat. To be honest, I don't really regret his failure to return and…claim me, so to speak."

"Oh, my dear, I did wonder about your grandfather's judgement at the time, but he had your best interests at heart. And the memory does play tricks as the years pass. Your own recollections might not be accurate."

"I suppose so. You mentioned you had an idea in relation to the portrait, Lady M?" Yet again, she brought the old lady back to the subject in question.

"Yes, I did. There's a sale coming up. It was advertised in yesterday's paper. I should have thought to carry it through from the drawing room. Let us return there."

Back in the drawing room, they found the folded broadsheet lying on one of the sideboards. Lady Millicent picked it up and laid it on the table next to the sofa.

"Here it is, on the front page," she said, holding her quizzing glass up to her stronger eye. "*Sale of unfinished paintings and sketches in oil, chiefly portraits of nobility and ladies of fashion by John Hoppner Esq RA*. It's to be held at Mr Christie's sale room at 83 Pall Mall."

"I suppose his widow needs funds," Cordelia commented. "How can this help us? It says *unfinished* works. They might not want completed items included."

Lady Millicent returned to studying the notice in the paper. "There are some complete works in the sale as well. It mentions a few pictures by Sir Joshua Reynolds and some by Thomas Whitcombe—he's that well-known naval artist, but Reynolds' work is bound to be portraits, so they might consider including ours. The sale is tomorrow se-ennight and the catalogue is not printed until a few days beforehand. Let us at least call in at Mr Christie's sale room and enquire. We might combine it with our outing to obtain my new veil."

"But that's twice as far as Bond Street," Cordelia exclaimed. "I think we must stretch to paying for a hansom cab." It was not on her own account that she suggested this. Rather, she feared the old lady would struggle to walk so far.

Lady Millicent pursed her lips in not quite a smile. "A compromise. Let us walk to Bond Street first and then obtain a cab for the onward journey to Pall Mall. The fare will certainly be a worthwhile investment if it results in funds. Let us get going. Are you certain you won't mind disposing of the portrait in this way."

"Not at all. I have no feelings for the man and I doubt we'll ever see him again." Of more concern to Cordelia was that Lady Millicent might be overdoing things. It was not only the extension of today's outing to include Pall Mall, but the lady's plans for the following day. The two were connected, for a lady could not in all conscience attend a funeral without wearing a veil. "Are you certain you wish to walk all the way to the embankment to watch this funeral procession tomorrow morning, on top of today's outings? I expect half of London will be trying to do the same."

"You're probably right, but I feel I must. Many of the crowd, like me, will recall the man's earlier life as a barrister and the way he defended Princess Caroline against those awful accusations by the Prince of Wales. Then, again, it's not every day a Prime Minister gets assassinated. I doubt such a terrible event will occur again in my lifetime, or even in yours. I feel I must be there to pay tribute to the man. He was such a good Christian soul. You are not to worry. I received a note from Dowager Countess Cholmondely yesterday. She will take me in her carriage. She assured me it would be no trouble, being just across the square as she is. They will call for me at eight. The procession's due to leave Downing Street at nine."

2: Encounter in Bond Street

A Friday morning early in the summer season, it appeared, was a far from sensible time to be negotiating Bond Street. The pavement might be of a generous width, but it seemed the whole of fashionable society was bent on shopping there today. It did not help Captain Henry Stanhope's cause that he carried a sailor's bag on one shoulder and was attempting to walk abreast with his two naval companions, who were likewise encumbered.

In the end it became easiest to proceed in single file, with Henry in front. His gold braided captain's coat and matching bicorne hat apparently drew respect and caused other pedestrians to steer a course around them. At least, that was true until he reached a particular ladies' clothing shop. From the display visible through the large window, it looked like a fairly exclusive establishment. He was almost level with the shop door, when a somewhat substantially-built and quite elderly lady stepped out directly in his path, forcing him to halt and causing James Hutcheson, directly behind him, to bump into Henry and Christopher Garvey in turn to do the same to James.

No one moved for a moment. Henry was about to speak to the woman and ask if she was all right. He knew he'd not actually touched her but she was possibly a little shocked by the encounter. It seemed she was definitely so, for her pale eyes were wide and the pupils dilated as she quite stared at him, her mouth seemingly trying to form words but uttering no sound.

Another woman stepped from the shop, middle aged and petite and, as he soon detected, French.

"Oo la la, Madame," she said. "Votre baton! La rue est passante." She handed over the stick and slipped her hand around the lady's free arm and proceeded to guide her through the passing throng to the edge of the pavement, where she hailed a hansom cab. The old lady allowed herself to be led, but twisted her pearl-encrusted neck so she continued to stare at Henry. Had she not had her stick in one hand and the

French maid hanging onto her other arm, she might well have come to grief.

For his part, Henry had been so busy watching the two ladies that he'd failed to notice a third member of the party.

"Oh, do wait for me," cried a petulant voice, before the owner of it crashed right into him. By then James and Christopher had stepped aside to observe the entertainment now developing before their eyes.

"Are you all right, miss," he addressed the bundle in a green muslin pelisse, as he disentangled himself.

"Huh! A sailor. I might have known it. No manners! You should address me as *my lady*," she retorted, as she stepped back and brushed her clothing straight. "And no, I am not all right. I am quite shaken about. Why don't you look where you're going?"

That was rich, given that she'd clearly stepped out of the shop without looking herself, but one didn't argue with a lady, he supposed. He was about to speak the words of apology that were evidently expected, if not actually justified, when he found the young woman, having finished smoothing down her skirts, was now focused on his face. It was astonishing. She looked quite lost for words and was examining his visage thoroughly, feature by feature, rather as the old lady in purple had. She only looked away when that same lady summoned her.

"Come Cordelia, we've not got all day. The cab won't wait."

Without another word, Cordelia—or rather, the Lady Cordelia—turned up her nose, adjusted the reticule hanging from her wrist and dodged the various pedestrians in her path to reach the edge of the pavement. There she stood for a while, looking up at the cab. Henry sensed she was reluctant to climb in. Then it was as if she took a deep breath and squared her shoulders, before taking a grip with both hands and mounting the step. But before she took her seat, she glanced over her shoulder in his direction and a frown creased that rather pretty face. What possessed him, he couldn't imagine, for after all he didn't know the lady. He raised his hat and gave a solemn bow. By the time he was upright again, she'd disappeared inside and the cab was rolling away.

"Well Captain Hal," James said, "if that's the measure of the kind of young lady to be met with in London's summer season, I can see why you wish to spend it here. I begin to be sorry to be heading north to visit my parents. What say you, Doc?" He turned to Christopher Garvey, who was ship's surgeon under Henry's command, while James was ship's master. The three of them had developed a firm friendship over the past few years of serving on the same ship and, all being single gentlemen, had gravitated together on this enforced leave. Christopher was the eldest of the trio, at thirty-five, as well as over six feet in height, with golden good looks and the kind of physique and face that drew female attention like a magnet. James, at twenty-five, was the junior member of the trio. His fair hair was bleached by the sun, which brought out the freckles in his complexion, and he had a cheerful disposition.

"I, on the other hand, shall be spending at least a month in Town," Christopher said, "so I shall watch developments with interest."

"There's Steven's Hotel up ahead," Henry said, desirous of changing the subject. That had been a strange encounter. Both the old lady and the young Cordelia had examined him in such a way that implied they recognised him, while for his part, he was certain they'd never met before. The only occasions on which he'd been in London over his ten years of naval service had been for brief stays in the dockland area, when a ship was in for repairs or re-provisioning. He'd never attended any society events, even on his rare visits to his father's estate in Wiltshire.

The hotel lobby was almost as busy as the street and the three of them had a wait of some quarter-hour before being attended to by the desk clerk. Henry was glad he'd sent his attorney that express from Portsmouth instructing the man on various matters, including reserving three rooms at Steven's Hotel. He'd not stayed here before, but it was said to be a convivial place at which to reside when in Town and popular with both army and navy officers.

"Good day to you, gentlemen," the man at the desk greeted them at last. "Captain…?" he queried as he met Henry's eye.

"Stanhope," he replied, "and my colleagues Mr Hutcheson and Mr Garvey."

The clerk checked his book and nodded. "All in order," he said. "If you'd like to sign the register."

Henry did so first and then engaged the man in conversation.

"You're extremely busy, as is Bond Street—as crowded as a ship's deck on muster."

"Indeed, sir, as is every hotel in Town as well as the shops, most of which will be closing tomorrow as a mark of respect, so they're keen to do good trade today. 'Tis not every day we see a Prime Minister buried."

"What! Perceval is dead? When did that happen?"

"Ah, you've been away at sea."

"Yes. We docked at Portsmouth a few days ago and immediately caught another ship to London."

The clerk nodded sagely. "I'm guessing the news hadn't reached everywhere by then. It only happened on Monday—four days ago."

"We'd not heard news he'd been ill."

"Nor was he, sir. Not until an assassin's bullet caught him and made him very sick indeed. There's a funeral procession tomorrow to carry him from Downing Street to Charlton for burial—it's where he grew up, apparently. I expect half of London will line the route. The dastardly assassin was put on trial this morning. No doubt they've already sentenced him to the gibbet. There's no question but he did it."

"Thank you for the information, we may well pay our respects."

Later, in the bar, the three of them heard more about the awful event. Everything was being done with great despatch and rumours abounded. Had the man worked alone? Was it a conspiracy? There was certainly disaffection across the poorer sections of the population. The ongoing war required taxes and trade blockades, which made prices of essentials too high for the poor on the one hand and reduced essential imports on the other.

The three of them knew all too well about that, for had not the *Europa* spent the past few years capturing French and Spanish ships, a far more popular employment with the crew than ferrying troops back and forth to the Peninsular, which they'd also had their share of. With captured cargo and even entire vessels, came the prizes from which all members of the crew benefited. Such successes over a number of years had feathered Henry's own nest and, with his attorney's help, he'd invested the income wisely. But he kept that aspect of his life private. Neither of his friends was aware he owned a villa in Surrey as well as several valuable paintings that adorned its walls.

Before they retired for the night, James Hutcheson, ever enterprising when routes were to be planned, showed them the map he had sketched out.

"What's this, Hutch?" Christopher joked. "Going to run conducted tours about Town?"

"Only as far as Westminster Bridge. I'm told that will be the best vantage point for watching the funeral procession and it's not too far to walk there." He spread out the map on the table between them. "See, it comes along Whitehall and turns for the bridge here, so if we stand around this point, we'll get a close view of the carriages as they make the turn onto the bridge."

"Won't everyone else have the same idea?" Henry said.

"Probably…which is why I suggest we retire now and rise with the sun. I doubt anyone else will be about and we can take a leisurely walk through St James's, cross the park to Birdcage Walk and follow the road along to the bridge." He pointed out the route on his sketch map as he spoke. "There'll be no carriage traffic to bother us, since no one but the royal family is permitted to drive along the Walk and I doubt they'll rise that early. Besides, I've heard there will be no royal attendance. The Prince Regent has consented to make provision for Perceval's widow and children, but I don't think there was any love lost, not since the Princess Caroline fiasco."

"Oh, yes, I recall it," Doc said. "Some six years ago, now. I was on leave and was kept very entertained by the newspaper accounts of the time. The poor lady was accused of bearing an illegitimate child and it was Mr Perceval who conducted, as it was referred to at the time, a *delicate investigation*. He ruled there was no case to answer."

"I hardly think anyone would have blamed her if the finding had gone the other way," Henry commented, "given how many offspring her princely husband has fathered on the wrong side of the blanket."

Early the following morning, not long after the three comrades had set out, it became clear that either someone had stolen Hutch's map and shared it quite widely, or a considerable proportion of the population had come up with a similar plan. Nevertheless, on reaching the end of Bridge Street, they were able to take a stance behind a row of aristocratic ladies, seated on chairs, each with a servant standing behind holding a parasol to protect their heads from the sun. Fortunately, none of the servants was that tall, so their view was unimpeded.

After a while the deepest bell at Westminster Abbey began its slow mourning toll, signalling that the procession must now be leaving Downing | Street. The watching crowd fell silent and waited.

At last, the front riders made the turn onto the bridge, immediately followed by the black-draped hearse. Henry caught a glimpse of the pinched, white face of the late Prime Minister's eldest son, who was only seventeen and thrust into the position of chief mourner in the coach immediately behind the hearse. He overheard a remark made by one of the seated ladies in front of them, to her neighbour.

"Of course, the chief victims in such an event are the widow and children—thirteen of them we're told and all so young." Her strident tone sounded familiar.

"I feel for her," the other lady replied, "especially as convention does not allow her to be present. But it would possibly have been too much for the poor, bereaved lady to cope with."

"And just see what they're putting that poor young man through," the first lady said. Surely his uncle could have been chief mourner instead."

Henry felt heartily sorry for the young man, also called Spencer, and quietly murmured "Hear! Hear!"

The lady nearest him evidently had sharp hearing, for she pushed aside the arm of the servant holding the parasol and swivelled her jewel-encrusted neck to examine him. "The gentleman from the navy agrees with me, Millicent. I must have sound judgement."

"Whom do you mean?" Millicent replied, as she also dispensed with her sun-protection and turned to examine him.

Good heavens, Henry thought, twice in as many days. It was the purple-clad lady from the Bond Street modiste's shop. She wore a veil this morning, but there was no mistaking the outfit, nor the triple ring of pearls, nor the voice. Henry, who wore no headgear, having removed his hat as the procession began to pass, could see he'd been recognised too and the old lady was frowning, as she had before, perhaps trying to place him amongst her acquaintance, but failing to do so. He was certain they had not encountered one another before yesterday.

Nothing more was said and the parasols were duly repositioned. At last, the tail end of the procession, which consisted of over thirty carriages and more than twice as many horses, rolled by. Moving at such a slow pace meant plenty of equine deposits along the way and a gang of street boys was beginning to sweep them up. The level of chatter amongst the on-lookers rose and the crowd began to disperse. The row of grand ladies remained seated to wait for their drivers, who each had to negotiate their turn to pull up beside the pavement to collect them. That included the lady in purple and her friend, who began another conversation, unaware that he was still behind them and could hear every word.

"Who was that man—the navy captain?"

"What did you say, dear?" the purple Lady Millicent replied. She was evidently a little deaf.

The first lady repeated the question in a considerably louder voice and even Hutch and Doc heard it this time and gave him a questioning look. He shrugged.

"I'm not sure, Margaret. He looks...but I tell myself it can't be. He's too young."

Henry decided to clarify the matter. He had no idea just whom they thought he was, but a few words from him would clear the matter up.

"Excuse me, ladies," he began and paused while they had their parasols lowered. "I could not help but overhear you. My name is Captain Stanhope and I have lately returned from the war on His Majesty's Ship *Europa*." He gave a slight bow before turning to his two friends. "Shall we?" he said, indicating with the sweep of one hand, their return route.

Inevitably, Henry was roundly teased by the two other men as they retraced their steps back to the hotel.

"So, the grand lady Millicent has her eye on you, Hal," Hutch said.

"What nonsense," Henry told them both. "I've never met her before—apart from almost bumping into her yesterday."

"Well, it might be an acquaintance worth cultivating, if you want to meet that rather delectable little piece she had with her yesterday," Doc said.

Henry laughed. "Ha...you mean the French maid?"

"You know perfectly well I do not."

"Oh, the other one," Henry said. "The snooty Lady Cordelia. I'll leave her to you, though if her father's anything like King Lear, I'd steer well clear, if I was you."

"Did you happen to notice the young lady's skirt, yesterday," Doc asked them. "I caught a glimpse as she ran for the cab—covered in frogs it was. If your suit fails, Hal, she can always hope one of them might metamorphosise into a prince!"

Henry laughed, but Hutch decided to change the subject, perhaps having grown bored with the current topic, since he was heading north in a few days, so would not be around to witness whatever fun might transpire in the courting of the Lady Cordelia.

"Now then, you two old salts, I have but four days remaining in Town before I catch the post north. Any thoughts on what we might do?

"Death somewhat whets my appetite," Doc said. "I plan a little local sport this evening. Bond Street furnishes several suitable hostelries I believe."

"Take good care, my friend," Henry said, thinking the man was somewhat remiss at failing to follow the very advice he was ever giving the sailors in his care.

"Worry not, Hal, they're guaranteed clean, for which one pays, naturally."

Turning then to James Hutcheson, Henry suggested an alternative. "Fancy another type of sport, Hutch? We could book a fencing session. As to other entertainments, a quick look at the society page in the *Morning Post* should furnish sufficient opportunities in which to indulge. I'm sure there'll be a copy in the hotel."

On duly consulting it over dinner, Henry was surprised to see so many society events listed. It was business as usual, so far as the *haut ton* was concerned. Expectations of some period of national mourning were clearly unfounded.

Doc took up the paper. "Spoilt for choice, by the looks of it," he told them. "There's something every day of the week, most with several to choose from."

"Does one require an invitation?" Hutch asked.

"I don't see why," Doc said. "I think we could simply turn up. Why else do they publish the address and the start time?"

"I've never been privileged to participate in a season myself," Henry told them, "but I recall one of my older brothers mentioning one requires vouchers to attend a ball at Almacks. Apart from that, I think it's a general free-for-all. The measure of success of these events depends, I believe, on how many hundreds of guests the hostess can squeeze in the door and how many of these are royalty or nobility. They list them by title in the paper. I doubt they sink so far as to mention naval captains, masters or surgeons, however."

"Shall we try our luck, then," Doc suggested. "There's only one event listed for tomorrow. It's something called a conversazione and it's held every Sunday throughout the season. Says it begins at three, with supper at five. That will leave the evening free for…other activities."

"Sounds like a conversation," Hutch said. "Where is it?"

The hostess is the Dowager Countess Cholmondely and she lives in Berkeley Square."

Hutch extracted his map from his jacket pocket and consulted it. "Conveniently close to Bond Street," he told them. "About ten or fifteen minutes' walk I'd say. Shall we go in uniform, Hal?"

"It gives us some credentials, I imagine. We'd best have them sponged down and pressed."

"Ditto my evening suit, I suppose," Doc said. As a surgeon, he wore his own civilian clothes on board ship.

3: A society gathering

Sunday 17th May 1812, Berkeley Square

"Do we have to attend the countess's Conversazione this afternoon, Lady M? It will be so boring."

"Well, Cordelia, I get the impression the countess rather wants us to be there. I think she's keen to ensure a good turnout, being the first one of the season. It's not every Sunday she insists on giving us a ride in her carriage to attend morning worship at St George's, as well as taking the trouble to bring us back home again afterwards."

"Well, she does only live across the square, which makes it very little inconvenience for her."

The grand lady had dropped them back at home a short while ago and the two of them were now sharing a pot of tea in the drawing room.

"Did she mention what the topic is today?" Cordelia asked.

"She did. In considerable detail. You can't have been paying attention. It's to be a talk by Sir George Mackenzie, the explorer. He'll be describing his recent travels in Iceland, although between you and me, I imagine he's hoping for orders for his recently published book on the topic. It costs three guineas, the countess informed me, and that's only for volume one. However, it is filled with engravings of what he saw there. No doubt he'll have some copies to show us, not that *we* can afford to purchase one."

"But what am I supposed to wear?" Cordelia went on. "There are bound to be a lot of fashionable people present."

"Put on that pretty Chinese silk pelisse over one of your plain white muslin dresses. If you keep the pelisse fastened all the way up the front, no one will see what you're wearing underneath. I can find you a nice silk rose to fix in your hair. You'll look quite fine."

Every objection Cordelia tried to voice was batted away by the insistent Lady Millicent. There remained the mystery of why the countess had been so keen for them to attend. She got the sense there was another reason, apart from swelling the numbers.

With the exception of regular attendance at St George's in Hanover Square for Sunday worship, it had been a considerable time since Cordelia had attended any society gatherings and she owned to herself that she was a little nervous. Having dressed in accordance with Lady Millicent's advice, she stepped back from her dressing table and examined herself in the mirror. The cream silk pelisse fastened with a neck-to-hem row of satin-covered buttons, either side of which was embroidered a flowing leaf design in pale green satin applique and the overall effect was demure and neat.

You are the granddaughter of Lord Charles Elderfold, she told herself. Hold your head up high and don't let anyone treat you as lesser than you are. One thought came unbidden to her mind and she rather wished it had not. Would her uncle Harold or any of her other uncles be present this evening? Harold, as the eldest, was now Lord Elderfold and had been waiting a good few years to take possession of his father's house in Town. As long as Cordelia remained unwed, she had the use of it and Harold and his five brothers clearly wanted nothing to do with her. She knew they resented the arrangement made by their father, but really, it was not her fault.

Her reverie was interrupted by Adèle, who knocked and entered. "Madame dit dépêches toi."

Cordelia slipped her reticule over one wrist. It contained only a lavender-scented handkerchief. These events could be very crowded and a press of warm bodies in a confined space had consequences. She followed the maid downstairs.

"Ah, good," Lady Millicent greeted her. "Let us proceed. It's best to get there early if we want a seat near the front for the talk."

It only took a few minutes to walk round to the Dowager Countess Cholmondely's rather grand house on the west side of the square. Having seen her mistress safely up the front steps, Adèle disappeared below stairs while Cordelia took Lady Millicent's arm and escorted her into the enormous reception room which had been cleared of other furniture and filled with row upon row of rather uncomfortable-looking wooden chairs.

There had been no need to worry about attendance, for plenty of other guests were arriving now and there was only time to say a quick greeting to their hostess, before taking their seats right at the front. "I want to be able to hear the man," Lady Millicent insisted.

It took half an hour for all the seats to be filled. Once they were, the countess came forward to introduce Sir George, who then began his talk, speaking for a little short of an hour. Cordelia was surprised to find it quite interesting. The countess gave a vote of thanks and led her guests in applause.

"I suggest we all stand and move about after sitting still so long," she said. "Whilst you're doing that the chairs will be removed. Do mingle amongst yourselves. Supper will be served shortly. Sir George is happy to answer any questions you may have. He will also sign his book, for any of you wishing to purchase. There are some on the table here at the front and more at the back there."

Cordelia quite surprised herself. For, when Sir George stepped down from the raised lectern at which he'd spoken and looked around, he met her eye with a kindly smile and she found the courage to step forward.

"I have a question, sir."

"Yes, young lady. Ask away."

"May one swim in the geysers?"

"Mostly not. The temperature of the water is far too hot. In many cases if a body dived in without checking first, they'd be boiled alive. So it's not advised to try."

"Thank you, sir," Cordelia said, glad to have got her question in, for others were quite lining up now to ask more.

One was clearly a naval officer. He had on a smart navy-blue jacket, double breasted with brass buttons but otherwise quite plain. She heard him ask about navigation in the seas around Iceland and Sir George spoke of the hazards of icebergs at certain times of the year. As she listened, Cordelia gazed over the faces behind the naval man, all crowding round to listen, and almost gasped out loud. There he was again, that same naval officer who'd bumped into her in Bond Street and who so strongly resembled that portrait. He wore a similar style of jacket to the other man's, but his was covered in gold braid and had folded back white revers and a white satin waistcoat, above white trousers and highly polished black shoes. He looked very striking. As he listened, he gazed about and met her eye.

They stared at each other for a few moments and she could see his brows drawn together in puzzlement. Then she noted the colour of his eyes. They were blue and as bright as the summer sky! There was no way this could be the Marquess of Dartington. It was just one of those odd coincidences that he resembled the picture in most of his other features. She broke the eye contact and stepped back to Lady Millicent, who had remained in her seat.

"Would you like to stay here while I fetch you some supper, my lady?"

"That would be nice, dear. I'm not giving up my chair or I doubt I'll get it back."

Little did Lady Millicent realise Cordelia's true motivation. Far from being a generous act, it was a strategy to avoid having to go anywhere near the naval captain whom she felt still examining her. Cordelia studiously avoided looking his way again as she exited the room and made her way to the refreshment salon. Supper was quite a simple affair, with small plates containing a variety of tiny sandwiches. She collected one of these plus a glass of lemonade and turned to make her way through the crowd back to Lady Millicent. It took some time to steer a path without spilling the drink or losing the contents of the plate, for she was jogged several times.

Unlike Lady Millicent, Cordelia had very acute hearing. As ever, the guests crowding about the refreshment table, waiting their turn to be served, were sharing gossip and comment about fellow guests. Passing close to one such group, she sensed eyes following her.

"Surely, that's the footman's daughter," she heard a woman say. "She's not been seen in society for years."

"Except on her knees at St George's seeking forgiveness for her mother's sins," another woman said.

A man's voice joined in. "Well, that didn't prevent her engagement to the lecherous Dart."

"Indeed," said the first woman's voice. "Did you ever discover his real name?"

"No, but you can rest assured the trickster had no handle on it. Old Charles Elderfold was seriously taken in there."

"I heard..." began the second lady's voice, but Cordelia was now out of earshot.

At the threshold to the big room, she stood stock-still for a moment, repeating in her mind what she'd just heard. They must have been talking about her, for Dart was the abbreviation she remembered hearing used several times in relation to the Marquess of Dartington. Those people she'd just overheard, whoever they were, were accusing him of being a fraud, who'd tricked her grandfather and wasn't a Marquess at all. That part about her engagement to the Marquess of Dartington made sense, but what about the first comment, the one she'd not really taken in because it had meant nothing to her. The woman who spoke first had referred to her as *the footman's daughter* and that she attended church to pray for her mother's sins! What was that about? Would Lady Millicent know? She must find an opportunity to ask her.

Meanwhile she must deliver the refreshments. A glance about the room told her the two naval men and another taller man with them were making their way towards her along the left-hand side, so she took the opposite route, ensuring she was hidden behind several groups of people standing about. She would not attempt to repeat the trek to the refreshment room for herself, so she would simply have to go hungry and wait until they returned home to quench her thirst.

"Thank you, Cordelia," Lady Millicent said, balancing her glass on the plate and beginning to nibble the sandwiches.

There were no other chairs left, except one or two around the edge of the room similarly occupied by older guests like Lady Millicent. Cordelia stepped over to the nearby table, where copies of Sir George's book could be viewed. She opened one and flipped through some of the illustrations. The etchings were certainly very fine. She found one showing the great geyser erupting like a volcano, except it was apparently all hot water and steam. She was turning to the next page, when a man's voice spoke.

"May I offer you some refreshments, my lady? It's a considerable squash to join the queue again."

It was him! The naval captain. She turned to find him holding an identical offering to that she'd just delivered to Lady Millicent. He was several inches taller than her five foot six and was gazing down at her with a slight smile, his brows raised in enquiry. She recalled being a little rude to him in Bond Street. How should she respond? It was not really proper for him to approach her like this.

"That's very kind of you, sir...captain...but we've not been introduced."

"Let me put that right at once. The one nearest you, on white bread, is cucumber, next to that I believe is—"

"What nonsense," she interrupted, trying to retain a serious expression, when she really wanted to laugh. He was quite funny.

"We could disturb your companion over there," he said, indicating Lady Millicent. "She could make the introduction. However, she seems to be in somewhat earnest conversation with that other lady in the blue dress.

Cordelia glanced across. A woman she did not recognise was standing beside Lady Millicent's chair, bending close to the old lady's ear. Whatever she was saying, Lady Millicent did not look particularly pleased with the encounter. She was frowning and shaking her head.

"You have been introduced to Lady Dunwoody?" Cordelia asked the naval captain, all astonishment.

"In a manner of speaking. We shared a section of pavement at Westminster Bridge yesterday morning. She and this evening's hostess thought I was someone else, so I put matters right by giving them my name."

"Let me guess. They thought you were the Marquess of Dartington."

"Perhaps they did. No name was mentioned, but I assured them, as I assure you now, I am Captain Henry Stanhope of His Majesty's Navy…at your service." He tipped his head in the hint of a bow, without breaking eye contact. "Now please accept my offering, before my wrists grow tired and I drop it, cucumber sandwich and all, on the floor"

What could she do but accept?

"Thank you."

"And I believe you go by the name Cordelia."

"Oh…how did you know that?"

"I heard you summoned on Bond Street, by your companion there. So you are the Lady Cordelia Dunwoody?"

"Oh…no, actually. I'm a Penshurst. Lady Dunwoody is my…er…chaperone, I suppose, but I'm actually the granddaughter of the late Lord Charles Elderfold."

"You have a complicated family. Shall I fetch you a chair, my lady, or maybe I should find one for myself?" he asked her.

That made her smile. "No, thank you, but do go ahead." She was so thirsty, she tipped the glass to her mouth and downed the lemonade in one go and deposited the glass beside Sir George's books on the table, before beginning to tackle the sandwiches. Captain Stanhope's lips were pursed in amusement. She *was* being a little unladylike. Having made short work of said cucumber sandwich she proffered the plate his way. "May I interest you in a sandwich, captain? I believe the one nearest you is ham and tomato."

"No thank you. They're all yours. I had an early dinner at our hotel."

Suddenly, Cordelia became aware of Lady Millicent's voice. She had no idea who the woman in the blue dress was, but it was clear their discussion had become somewhat heated and she could not fail to hear the way Lady Millicent drew the encounter to a close. Nor could the captain.

"I don't believe we've anything further to say to each other, Florence." With that, Lady Millicent pushed herself up from her chair, took hold of her walking stick and began looking for Cordelia, while the other woman raised her chin and, with a disapproving sniff, walked away.

"Oh good, you're here," Lady Millicent said, on spotting her. "Time to go. Fetch Adèle."

"Of course," Cordelia said, although she was rather loath to walk away from the handsome captain.

Only then did Lady Millicent recognise the man with whom Cordelia had been talking. "Good heavens, the man from Westminster Bridge," she said. "Captain Stanhope, is it not?"

So they really had been introduced. As Cordelia set off to find Adèle, she heard his response. "It is indeed. May I be of assistance, my lady?"

Cordelia found the maid in the servants' hall.

"Come Adèle," she instructed in a firm voice. "Her ladyship is ready to depart."

It soon became clear that the maid was in no state to take Lady Millicent's arm for the short walk round the square to home, for she had evidently enjoyed a party of her own and lemonade had most definitely not been her liquor of choice. How was Cordelia to manage both of them?

Back in the lobby she found the answer, for Lady Millicent was on the arm of Captain Stanhope! The old lady raised her brows at the sight of Adèle, whose balance was wavering somewhat, and addressed Cordelia.

"This kind gentleman has offered his arm to escort me home, Cordelia. Perhaps you could do the same for our French friend? Ah, Margaret, my dear, there you are. Thank you so much for such an interesting time. Do you remember our gallant friend from yesterday, Captain Stanhope?"

"I do indeed," the countess said. "So glad you could join us, Captain. I'll ensure you and your two friends receive an invitation for the next one."

That told Cordelia they must have inveigled their way in without one on this occasion! Other guests were also wanting to depart now and it was impossible for her to get near enough to the countess to say her farewells, so Cordelia, who was having a little difficulty with Adèle, had to wait her turn. When at last she made her curtsy to their hostess, she could not see Lady Millicent and her escort anywhere. They must have set out already. The countess drew Cordelia to one side and whispered in her ear.

"Rumours are flying, my dear. They're saying your captain is the flighty Dart returned, having reinvented himself as a naval officer. His escorting Lady Millicent home will only add weight to that conclusion."

Cordelia was astonished. "Impossible my lady. He would be over forty by now and I doubt our chivalrous captain has seen his thirtieth birthday yet. Besides—"

The countess interrupted her. "Don't be a fool, Cordelia. You're what, four-and-twenty now? What other chance might come your way. They say he's very rich and he may be a youngest son, but his father's a viscount. It might be wise *not* to contradict the rumours. I had hoped some mending might be encouraged with your Uncle Harold and Aunt Florence, who were present tonight, but unfortunately all that resulted was something of a scene between Florence and Millicent, so it came to naught. Good night, my dear. Remember what I said."

Cordelia had much to occupy her on the short walk home. Practically speaking her principal task was to keep Adèle upright. She was frustrated not to be able to catch up to Lady Millicent and the captain, so as to eavesdrop on their conversation. On reaching their front door, she found the gentleman politely refusing an offer to come into the house and bowing his goodnight. He did the same to Cordelia, but said nothing, except his failed attempt to hide a smirk evidenced his amusement at her antics with the maid. Then he strode off in the direction of Bond Street.

"Get Adèle to the kitchen and tell cook to brew her some strong coffee," Lady Millicent instructed Cordelia. "And have a tea-tray sent up to the drawing room. I wish to talk with you."

Cordelia suddenly recalled that conversation she'd overheard when making her way from the refreshment room. In all the confusion of dealing with Adèle she'd quite forgotten. She very much wished to talk to Lady Millicent as well.

What Lady Millicent had to say to Cordelia was not dissimilar to what the countess had said.

"It's ridiculous," Cordelia responded. "He's far too young to be the marquess and his eyes are the wrong colour."

"You and I know that, my dear girl, but the general population of the *haut ton* does not. This could be the answer to all our problems. He told me he's on leave for a few months while his ship undergoes repairs. Unfortunately, he goes away tomorrow to visit the widow of a naval lieutenant who served with him, but he will be back towards the end of the week. We must discover which society events he will be attending and be sure to gain invitations."

"I don't see the point of that, Lady M. For all we know, the man may already be betrothed." A thought she did not add was how inadequate she felt to put herself about in such a way. She had no confidence as to how to behave in society and nor did she have anything suitable to wear. A man like the handsome captain would have no interest in an innocent like her, but let Lady Millicent enjoy her fantasies. She wouldn't argue.

"Let us take it a day at a time," Lady Millicent said.

"Before we retire, Lady M, may I ask you something? Why should I be referred to in society as the *footman's daughter*?"

There was utter silence, broken only by the clock on the mantel striking the quarter hour. Cordelia stared at Lady Millicent, who in turn stared back.

"Ah," the old lady said, at last looking away. "I knew you'd have to be told one day." She paused, as if trying to find the words. "It was cruel of those other guests to gossip in your presence like that."

"Well?" Cordelia prompted, meeting the old lady's gaze once more.

"You know your mother was the long-awaited daughter, after the six boys who came before her. I'm sorry to say she disgraced herself and the family by…eloping with one of the servants. Footman Penshurst. They found a priest to say the words, but there was some doubt as to whether it was valid. Nevertheless, you took his name. But then there was the carriage accident. You were so young. Your dear grandfather vowed you should not suffer for your parents' misbehaviour and you came to live here and he changed his will to give you security until you wed."

Cordelia said nothing for a moment, as she gathered her thoughts. She sighed.

"I suppose I should be shocked, but somehow it doesn't come as much of a surprise. I knew there must be a reason for the estrangement with all my uncles."

Lady Millicent nodded, her expression sad. "And I doubt there'll be a mending there. Your eldest uncle and his wife were present this evening and the wife quite accosted me."

"The woman in the blue brocade gown?"

"Yes. She said I had no right to be there, nor to bring you."

Cordelia thought, but did not say out loud, that her somewhat humiliating circumstances also explained why Grandpapa had jumped at agreeing the alliance with the Marquis of Dartington. Evidently, he'd been willing to take her despite her unfortunate background. She could do nothing about the fact that her history was generally known in society. Lady Millicent had not thought it through, but Cordelia saw the problem at once.

"Lady M, I think I should point out that it is hardly likely your gallant captain would wish to align himself with the possibly illegitimate daughter of a footman. I gather his father is a viscount, who would surely never countenance such an alliance."

4: An auction

Saturday 23rd May 1812, Pall Mall

It had not been Henry's intention to escort Mrs Frances Williams to Town after calling upon her a few days ago. His visit to the village, just into Kent, where she was now residing with her brother and his wife, had been a courtesy one. His purpose had been to express his condolences at the death of Lieutenant Williams, some six months ago now. From a selfish point of view, it had also been an ideal opportunity to try out the carriage and pair his attorney had, as instructed, obtained for him. The brass-mounted curricle had cost him sixty guineas, including the harness, but that was nothing compared to the two seven-year-old matched-greys to pull it, which together had set him back more than twice as much.

Henry had stayed a few nights to enjoy a little local walking in the very pretty countryside thereabouts. He'd made the mistake of mentioning this to the brother as well as revealing that he would be travelling back to Town on Friday for commitments on Saturday. He suspected Mrs Williams had previously had no intention of visiting Town, until his turning up unexpectedly had provided her with the opportunity of free transport and it would have been churlish to refuse her request.

Several things concerned him about Mrs Williams sharing his carriage back to Town. Did the lady have expectations? He'd never met her before, but suspected she might indeed have designs on him. Her brother and sister-in-law had a young family and a small cottage and, although Henry had stayed at the local inn during his visit, the brother had pressed him to dine with them each evening. No doubt, they hoped Frances would soon find her own establishment, so they possibly had expectations also. There had been several remarks such as *how kind of you to take such trouble to come all this way* from the lady herself. From the sister-in-law, when observing Frances playing with her youngest child, quietly commenting to him *she would make such a good mother.* And from the brother, *I think my sister is very open to making another match.* In juxtaposition to remarks about his own single status, they were telling indeed. Frances Williams was a very pretty woman, only about five-and-twenty years of age and one would need to be blind not to notice she had, as they said, a glad eye.

Now he had endured a two-hour ride in the close confines of a two-seater curricle with no maid as chaperone. Only the fact of her widowed status and the formality of his naval uniform saved him from being thought something other than a gentleman. At least the weather was fine enough to drive with the hood folded back, making the innocence of such close proximity obvious to any observers. There were no clasped hands or clandestine kisses.

He experienced considerable relief on at last crossing Westminster Bridge. His duty would soon be done.

"Your brother said you intended staying in Mayfair," he said. "Where may I deliver you, so to speak?"

"Oh, I'm not sure. I've not booked anything. I wasn't certain how long I'd be away. Where do you suggest?"

"I'm not that familiar with what might be appropriate…er…given you have no maid accompanying you. The Clarendon, perhaps?"

"Goodness, I doubt I can afford that. Where are *you* staying, Henry?"

Thus far in their brief acquaintance, Henry had addressed the lady as Mrs Williams and she had called him Captain Stanhope. They had not progressed on to the intimacy of first names.

"Steven's, in Bond Street," he said, trying to keep the annoyance he was feeling out of his tone. He'd well and truly fallen into this one. "But it's full of military personnel. I hardly think—"

"That will be just the thing," she said, interrupting him. "Why, I may even encounter others who remember my dear Samuel."

It occurred to Henry that the cost of residing at Steven's was probably little different to The Clarendon, but he made no comment.

"Of course, they may not have room," she added, "but perhaps we could try."

A glance her way showed Henry a somewhat pert, dimpled smile, which might have been thought sweet, had it not been for the gleam in those alert blue eyes. Henry wondered whether the brother and his wife had been party to this scheme of hers. How foolish to get himself into such an awkward situation, although he wasn't sure how he could have avoided it.

They soon pulled up outside Steven's and, naturally, Henry had to help her down and carry her bag into the lobby, where the clerk greeted him by name and looked enquiringly at his lady companion. Henry introduced her and explained her predicament of not having pre-booked anything.

That was quite sufficient explanation and the clerk was examining his register when Mrs Williams decided to add her own plea, in such a way that it gave the man little choice but to accommodate her, as well as giving him entirely the wrong idea about their relationship.

"Henry suggested it would be comforting to be amongst other naval officers. My dear husband passed away quite recently, you see. I do hope you have a room spare."

With a knowing glance at Henry the clerk smiled her way. "If you'd like to take a seat in the lounge, Mrs Williams, I'll have a tea tray sent through and see what I can do."

"Meanwhile," Henry said, "I must see to my horses. If you'd excuse me, Mrs Williams." He nodded at the clerk, who was smiling broadly and even gave him a wink! The man's amusement at Henry's attempt to sound formal with the lady, told him he had concluded the true situation was anything but innocent. Damnation!

On arriving at the livery stables around the corner, where he was hiring a stall for his horses, Henry decided to deal with removing the harness and rubbing down the animals himself. Not wishing to sully his best uniform, he stripped down to shirt and britches to complete the task, after which he washed under the tap in the yard, before dressing to return to the hotel. There was no sign of his erstwhile lady companion, but the clerk saw him and raised a hand to signal his attention.

"Excuse me, Captain Stanhope," the man said, "Mrs Williams asked me to tell you she's reserved a table for dining at six."

"Has she indeed?" Enough was enough. Henry decided to disabuse the man of his inaccurate assumptions. "I think I should make it clear that the lady and I are barely acquainted, certainly not to the extent whereby she should take the liberty of addressing me by my given name nor presume that I intend to dine with her. I certainly do not. I shall go to my room to change now and I am then out for the evening with my friends." He had no idea where Doc and Hutch were at this minute, but it was pretty certain they would have a social engagement somewhere and would surely return to the hotel beforehand to prepare. He intended joining them.

The clerk was looking somewhat uncomfortable—as he should, having over-stepped the bounds of civility with a customer. But apparently there was more to it than that.

"Ah…" he began and then hesitated. "Thing is, Captain Stanhope, the lady gave me to understand…that is…"

"What is it, man? Spit it out!"

"I had one of the other gentlemen moved to another room so Mrs Williams could occupy the one adjoining yours."

"I see. Well, no harm. The connecting door is locked. That was the first thing I checked."

The shame-faced clerk gave a nervous cough. "Well…um, actually, the lady requested the key."

There was utter silence for a full thirty seconds, but Henry did not need to put his thoughts into words. His expression said it all.

"I'm very sorry, Captain," the man stuttered. "The lady was very insistent."

"I'm sure she was. Well, here's what you are going to do. You will move the gentleman you previously inconvenienced—"

"Oh, he's out. He's not yet aware—"

"Even better. Move his possessions into my room and put me in his. It's up to you how you explain it, but I suggest you retrieve the key from the lady and make sure the door is locked. You can tell her I've moved out of the hotel for all I care!"

At that moment Henry's two friends entered the lobby.

"You're returned, Hal," Hutch said. "How was the grieving widow"

"You can buy me a large whisky in the bar and I'll tell you," Henry said, before scowling at the clerk and leading the way to a table well out of the sight of the lobby.

He was not surprised at their laughter when he told his tale.

"I hope you have some plans for this evening that will remove us from the vicinity," he said.

"Nothing fixed," Doc said. "There is a ball we could attend. It's only around the corner at Willis's Rooms."

"It's a masquerade," Hutch added. "Gives us an opportunity to assess the females present without being thought lewd."

"Does it not require a costume?" Henry asked.

"That's no problem," Doc said. "There's a hire shop in Strand, where they also sell tickets a lot cheaper than you pay at the door, though you pay for the costume hire of course. What say you?"

"I say, lead me to it," Henry replied. "Anything that gets me away from that predatory female."

"By the by," Doc asked, "is she aware of how her husband actually died?"

"I doubt it," Henry said. "I suspect she may eventually wonder why she's not being given financial compensation like other widows. At that point I imagine the authorities will have to explain. She asked me, of course. I was quite glad to be able to tell her that, given her husband was redeployed from our ship to a shore-based job some months before that sad event, I was not privy to the details concerning his death. In the circumstances, I thought a lie was advisable."

They found their chosen event went on all night and all three of them enjoyed the freedom of dancing anonymously with similarly masked young women, whom they could imagine were all beauties, just as their partners might in turn envisage them as handsome! Back at the hotel, they retired to their rooms around the same time as the day's milk was being delivered.

Henry's new room was at the back of the hotel on the second floor and he had quickly established an alternative exit route to avoid the main lobby. By using the back stairs down to the kitchens, he could escape via the back yard. It was unlikely he could evade Mrs Williams for ever, but at least by now she had received the message loud and clear that he was not her escort for this escapade of hers to Town.

The breakfast tray he'd ordered for noon duly arrived, along with a message that had been delivered from the Bond Street tailor he'd visited on first arriving in Town, to say that one of his coats and two sets of breeches were ready for a fitting. He was due at Christie's auction room by two. That should give him time to call in at the tailor's beforehand. If all was well, he would wear his new outfit to attend the auction.

Examining himself in the long mirror provided by the tailor, it was quite a surprise to take in the contrast to his normal apparel. The proprietor of this top-class establishment had informed Henry that dark fabrics were more in fashion at present, but that was too like his normal navy blue. Henry had insisted on this tan cloth for one of the coats. It was long-tailed, with the usual cut-away front, and was worn over a cream satin waistcoat embroidered in various shades of blue and brown. The shirt was a fine off-white linen and the outfit was completed with cream breeches, white stockings and his usual buckled black pumps plus, carelessly arranged about his neck, a white silk cravat. The shirt was ruffled at cuffs and neck but he had resisted an over-high collar and specified no lace at all. He had no intention of aping Beau Brummell. Nevertheless, observers would be hard-pressed to recognise him as the same figure who arrived at Steven's Hotel just a week ago.

"Ah," said the proprietor, "one more thing."

Henry found a black top hat being positioned on his head. It felt very strange after the softness of his naval hat, but he was pleased with the effect.

"Have my naval uniform packed up and returned to my hotel, if you please," he instructed the man, before setting off for Pall Mall.

Mr Christie operated from a substantial square room, which was more of a hall in dimensions, rising to a high-up canopy of small-paned windows which provided natural light and allowed the substantial area of wall-space below to be used for displaying pictures. There was already a crowd of potential customers occupying the central rows of bench seating, while others were standing around talking or examining the pictures on display. Henry scanned the room and soon spotted James Fagg. He was the highly efficient attorney who'd acted for Henry in various matters lately and would be bidding on his behalf today. They acknowledged each other with a slight nod of the head, but otherwise did not exchange any words of greeting.

A tall grandfather clock in one corner of the room chimed the hour and Mr Christie, a sheaf of papers in one hand, appeared from a side door and climbed up to stand at the lectern, which stood on a raised dais in the middle of the room. The chatter died away and an expectant hush took its place, with some rustling of paper as would-be bidders checked their catalogues. At this stage, one could not tell who was there to buy and who might be present to observe the outcome of something they were putting up for sale.

Proceedings soon began with a number of unfinished works by the late John Hoppner. Henry guessed from their garb that several of the young men bidding were students of art, keen to try their hand at completing a canvas or simply to own a work, albeit partial, by the late Academician and the items went relatively cheaply. Next came the sale of various portraits by Reynolds. Henry presumed they'd originally been painted for the sitter or a member of his or her family. Were they now being sold off to raise funds? He wondered what the point was in making such a purchase, if the subject was unknown to the purchaser? Perhaps it represented an investment, because of the artist's renown.

"Now we have a last-minute addition to our sale of portraits. This is another by the late Mr Hoppner—a completed one this time. The signature is authenticated. The sitter is unknown. It is the property of Lady Dunwoody. What am I bid?"

Henry was awaiting the naval paintings and was not paying much attention until he heard the name Dunwoody. She was the lady he'd escorted home on Sunday last following that Conversazione. He looked up from the catalogue he'd been perusing to examine the portrait the young attendant had just lifted onto the easel. Astonishing! That explained the way Lady Dunwoody and her young friend had examined his features so closely. It did resemble him remarkably, but was supposed to be of the elusive Marquess of Dartington. As far as Henry was concerned, there must be some mistake, for it could surely be none other than Henry's eldest brother Godfrey, as Henry recalled him shortly before Henry had left home to go to sea. He must have it!

There was utter silence in the room, and he quickly scanned it for any sense that he had a rival for the work. In so doing he spotted a young maid, in a black dress, white apron and mob cap, standing in a corner of the room, wringing her hands and looking anxious as she gazed at the portrait. He realised at once that she wasn't a maid at all, but the Lady Cordelia Penshurst in disguise. She must be there to witness the sale and this must surely represent the equivalent of selling off the family silver. They needed the money!

"Are there any bids?" Mr Christie prompted.

Henry had little time to think about it and he doubted he'd have any rival bidders to force the bids higher.

"One hundred guineas," he called out, raising one hand to draw attention to himself.

There was a collective gasp before an expectant hush and the gavel came down. "Sold to the gentleman in the tan coat."

By the time Henry turned round to check on Lady Cordelia's reaction, he could not see her. She'd evidently departed at once to give Lady Dunwoody the good news.

Across the room, James Fagg did meet his eye, his brows raised in enquiry. He must be surprised at Henry's unplanned purchase and be wondering if he still wanted to go ahead with what was bound to be a competitive auction for the Whitcombe painting he was after. Henry indicated by a brief nod that he did wish the man to go ahead. He knew he'd be forking out considerably more than he'd just spent on the Hoppner. While he still had Fagg's attention he also signalled that he was leaving. The man had his instructions so Henry didn't really need to stay. He went to the clerk's desk to give his details and agree arrangements for paying the hundred guineas and then made for the door. He wanted to catch up to Lady Cordelia before she reached home, if he could.

Outside, he guessed her most direct route would be up St James's Street and then to follow Berkeley Street to the square. It was not a happy thought. Four o'clock in the afternoon was the hour by which all the young ne'er-do-wells would have at last risen and set out for their evening's entertainment, which would be likely to include congregating at one or other of the so-called gentlemen's clubs, most of which were situated in St James's Street. He set off at a fair pace and as he turned off Pall Mall onto St James's, he saw her. She had already gone a considerable distance up the hill and was not alone. Four young men surrounded her and she looked very vulnerable, with her arms clasped protectively across her chest.

He set off at a run. By the time he reached the group, the tallest of the men was standing behind her, encasing her in a grip that pinioned her own arms against her, while another stood in front of her, far too close. The other two, who were a little younger, looked uneasy.

"Come on…only a kiss," said the one in front of her, his slurred speech evidencing his inebriated state. Not that it was any excuse, but it might make them easier to deal with.

5: Unexpected events

Cordelia couldn't wait to tell Lady Millicent the good news. Someone had bid one hundred guineas for that portrait of Dartington, not that they'd advertised it as such. It was not only a poor likeness, the man himself was a fraud, according to that gossip she'd overheard at Lady Margaret's Conversazione. She guessed the purchaser had bought it because it was a Hoppner, not because of the subject. She'd been concealed in one of the corners near the main door and had slipped out as soon as the gavel came down, so had not seen who made the bid, except he wore a tan-coloured coat.

This scheme to disguise herself as a maid and attend the auction had been thought up by Adèle, who'd lent her the outfit. Lady Millicent was anxious to hear the outcome as soon as possible because, as she repeatedly reminded them, they had creditors knocking on their door daily and she needed to be able to give assurances as to payment. The streets had been fairly quiet when Cordelia had set out. It was a different story now. As soon as she passed the first of those gentlemen's clubs and absorbed the lewd looks from the group of young men hanging about the entrance, she realised it had been a mistake to choose this route and an even bigger one to don this disguise, for were not housemaids thought easy pickings for the so-called gentlemen of the *ton*. She began to walk more quickly, head held high, pretending not to hear the suggestive comments from the next group she passed.

She was about half-way along, when she was accosted. A kiss, the man in front of her said, while another grabbed her from behind. She doubted that was all they intended, but surely they would not try anything more in broad daylight on the street? Her next thought was that they very well might, for she realised they were quite drunk and probably incapable of rational thought.

Then suddenly, in a flash of brown and cream, another man was there. He grasped the one in front of her by the arm and swung him to face his way and then immediately felled him with a fierce punch to his chin. Going behind the man who had her in such a tight grip, he forced his arms apart to release her and then gave him the same treatment. The other two men decided to retreat.

It was only when he gripped one of her hands and pulled her away that she realised it was Captain Stanhope, out of uniform. Astonishingly, his top hat was still on his head.

"Come, let's get you home."

He was wanting her to go a lot faster than she was capable of. Perhaps the shock of what had just occurred was beginning to take hold. Cordelia felt shaky and there were tears welling in her eyes.

"I c..c..can't," she said, "p..please slow down."

"Yes, you can, come on. We need to get round the corner into Piccadilly, where it's busier. I don't want to frighten you, but they've picked themselves up and they are actually coming after us."

Whether he'd intended it or not, that stimulated some extra effort from somewhere and together they ran around the corner. They were just short of Berkeley Street when the two men Captain Stanhope had hit caught them up.

"Hold up, there," one of them commanded. Captain Stanhope stopped and turned to face them, shielding her behind him.

Cordelia did not exactly see what happened next, but she heard it…the thwack of a kid glove being slapped against Captain Stanhope's face. By now various bystanders were gathering in a semi-circle around them to see what was happening.

"I don't think so, sir," the captain said. "Apart from being illegal, I am a captain in His Majesty's Navy and would forfeit my commission. Not that I wouldn't be willing to oblige you by running you through with a sabre, which is my weapon of choice, but I'm equally handy with a pistol, or with my fists, of course."

There was some nervous coughing from the two men and one of them spoke. "Ah, in that case, our apologies, captain, but may I point out that she's only a housemaid of some sort. Hardly worth making such a song and dance about it."

"Were you honourable men, you would believe it right to defend any woman's virtue, whatever her station in life. That being said, I feel I should warn you of the consequences of pursuing any vendetta against myself or this lady."

"Pah!" the second man exclaimed. "The only sensible consequence is that you accept our invitation to join in the fun."

"I think not. The only fun you're likely to enjoy is a spell in Newgate for molesting the granddaughter of Lord Charles Elderfold."

"What the devil?" said the first man. "But she's dressed as a maid!"

"Have you not heard of masquerades? It happens there was one last evening which lasted well into this morning. In fact, had you been there yourselves, you might well have unknowingly danced with this very lady. I seem to recall there were several with such a costume. Now I suggest we draw this unfortunate episode to a close, if you can find some manners through your inebriated fog."

Cordelia found herself suddenly exposed to the perusal of the two men as the captain stood aside and rested his hands on his hips. "Well?" he asked them. She tried to look calm and superior, as befitting a lady of the aristocracy, but to her consternation she was still trembling.

Neither of her attackers would meet her eye, but they did both give a somewhat token bow and muttered, "Apologies, my lady," before turning to retrace their steps. Before they disappeared around the corner, Cordelia was horrified, but hardly surprised, to hear what one said to the other. His voice was sufficiently penetrating for the audience that had accumulated around them to hear, as well as the captain, of course.

"Elderfold's granddaughter, hey? I've just realised who she is—the *footman's* daughter—remember the scandal?"

"No better than a housemaid, then," the other commented.

That set off murmuring amongst the bystanders. The captain took her hand again and led them across Piccadilly and into Berkeley Street. He said nothing, although he must surely be wondering what the men's parting comments had meant. By the time they'd reached Berkeley Square, she'd come to a decision.

"Might we take a turn about the gardens before I make for home?" she said.

"Of course." He let go her hand, opened the gate and led them in through the iron railings. He didn't take her hand again, as they walked side by side along the broad path, which went diagonally across, edged by flowering shrubs and ornamental trees.

This was one of the largest squares in Town and it would take them a good quarter hour to traverse it. Time enough, Cordelia decided, to relate her ignominious life history. She'd rather he heard it from her. However, Cordelia did not begin her explanation at once, because she suddenly took in what the captain was wearing.

"It was you!" she exclaimed. "You bought our picture."

"Ah…guilty as charged."

"But why? Although it does look a little like you."

He smiled and nodded. "Yes. I'd say it looks a lot like me. However, it looks a good deal more like my brother Godfrey. It's almost as if he sat for it. I understand it's supposed to portray the mysterious Marquess of Dartington."

"Neither Lady Millicent nor I have seen him for years, but our memories of his appearance are nothing like that picture. That's why we put it in the auction as an unknown subject. I'm so very grateful you purchased it, although I think you probably bid too high."

He shook his head. "If it does turn out to be the portrait my brother sat for years ago but which was never delivered, then it is worth a good deal more to the family than what I paid today. I do hope the funds will be of help."

"Oh they will indeed. We have considerable debts to pay off." She paused. "I owe you an explanation. Let me tell you how we became involved with the awful Dartington."

"There's really no need, unless you particularly want to."

"I do."

So she told it all, including the part she'd only recently learnt about the footman who'd fathered her. Walking side by side made it easier, for she didn't have to look him in the eye. She brushed quickly over the carriage accident that had killed both her parents and went on to relate her grandfather's misguided trust of the man calling himself Marquess of Dartington, who was probably nothing of the kind.

They reached the centre of the garden, where the two diagonal paths crossed, and paused beside the statue of King George the Third seated on a horse. The monarch's mount had legs that were somewhat spindly and it was said the precarious structure would soon require removal, before it fell down of its own accord, a metaphor for the sad state of the King's health at present, Cordelia thought, as well as for her own tenuous position in the Elderfold family. She found she could not meet the captain's eye.

"Cordelia," he said, facing her, his voice very quiet and gentle. "Look at me."

Reluctantly, she dragged her gaze to his face. His expression was serious, his brow furrowed.

"None of this is your fault, not how your parents behaved, nor the accident that brought you under your grandfather's guardianship, nor the inappropriate betrothal he allowed himself to be beguiled into. And society's tittle-tattle that has labelled you so unkindly is merely a measure of how shallow so-called high society can be. It was, perhaps, not a wise choice to go gallivanting about Town unescorted and dressed as a maid, but the actions of those so-called gentlemen were of their making, not yours."

"I prefer to walk when I can," she told him. "Besides I cannot really afford a cab."

He gave the hint of a smile then. "Can you afford the cost of a cup of tea? I don't know about you, but I could certainly manage one. Shall we?"

He offered his arm and she slipped hers into it. "Most definitely," she said. "And, thank you, Captain Stanhope." Her voice was still trembling, thinking of what could have happened this afternoon.

They completed their walk in silence and it was comforting to have his touch and to feel the warmth of the sunshine and hear the twittering of sparrows and see other residents of the square taking the air, although they did direct curious looks their way. It must seem odd, a finely clad gentleman apparently arm-in-arm with a humble housemaid!

On entering the house, they found Adèle pacing the hall floor and she greeted Cordelia in a torrent of French, amongst which she only caught a few words, but clearly something was wrong. It seemed the captain understood more.

"Lady Dunwoody is unwell? Where is she?"

The distraught woman pointed upstairs.

"Has a doctor been summoned?" the captain asked.

Adèle nodded. "Il est là." She pointed again.

"I must go to her," Cordelia exclaimed, at once rushing up the stairs and entirely forgetting her manners. She vaguely heard the captain conversing further with Adèle, but their voices faded as she rushed along the corridor to Lady Millicent's room at the back of the house. Outside the door, she paused and tried to compose herself by taking a few slow, deep breaths. Then she tapped on the door and quietly turned the knob.

The doctor was by the bedside, closing up his bag. He was the same man who'd attended Lady Millicent last time she'd taken a turn, as the old lady had put it.

"Ah, Adèle," he said, "is the Lady Cordelia returned?"

Only then did Cordelia realise how odd she must look. "Yes, I am!" she exclaimed, which caused the medical man to take a closer look.

"Good gracious, so you are. Why on earth are you dressed like that? Don't tell me Lady Millicent has had you scrubbing pots and pans?"

"Our household economy has not quite sunk to that, as yet. It's a long story, which I shan't bore you with. How is she?" It occurred to Cordelia that, if the man could make jokes, hopefully it might not be that serious. But as she watched, the smile rapidly faded from his face, to be replaced by a noticeable frown and she knew she was wrong.

"I'm afraid it's a little more serious this time. The apoplexy has resulted in some paralysis on her left side. It may be temporary, but I think you should face the fact that she is likely to be confined to bed for some time, and will need help feeding and with other…bodily necessities. I shall arrange a nurse."

"Is there any treatment, doctor?"

"We can do the usual bloodletting and administer some calomel, which is a type of purgative. Other than that, it's a matter of time and hope."

Cordelia asked no more, for the man's tone of voice told her he had little faith in the treatments he was proposing and there was probably very little hope of her recovery.

"She's sleeping now," he said. "Perhaps Adèle could sit with her, while you change out of your costume?"

"Yes, I ought to. May I offer you some tea, doctor?"

"That's kind, but I have another call to make. I shall visit again tomorrow."

Visiting twice in two days. This was serious! Not only that, but he'd have to be paid! By the time Cordelia had donned the first dress that had come to hand, that dull and dated muslin, she had entirely forgotten about Captain Stanhope! She sent Adèle up to sit with her mistress and it was only when she went down to the kitchen to update cook and the other two maids about the situation that she remembered—or rather that her attention was drawn to—his continued presence. It was cook who told her.

"I took the liberty of sending a tea tray up to the gentleman. He's in the drawing room, my lady."

"Oh…goodness me. I'd completely forgotten. Thank you. I'll go and…" She trailed off as she rushed up the service stairs.

She was astonished, on entering the drawing room, to find the captain standing by *Scarlet*'s cage, its cover in his hand, talking to the creature!

Who's a pretty boy, it squawked. Then it spied Cordelia and danced about on its perch. She feared she knew what was coming next. *Roger the moll!* Cordelia had heard this phrase before and was not quite sure what it meant, except it was probably very rude.

"I'll drown you in the drink if you don't behave yourself," the captain said, before throwing the cover back over the cage. He turned to greet Cordelia with a quick bow of the head. "How is she?"

Cordelia shook her head and felt tears welling. "Not good," she muttered through clenched teeth as she swallowed them away. The doctor's calling again tomorrow. Meanwhile he's sending a nurse."

"I'm so very sorry. How will you manage?"

They both knew to what he referred. Money was a delicate subject.

"I honestly don't know. Lady Millicent never involved me in financial matters. I doubt I could—"

"Nonsense," he interrupted. "You can do basic arithmetic, surely. And you can read and have an excellent command of English. If things are properly explained to you, I have no doubt you could manage affairs admirably."

"It's kind of you to say so, but I wouldn't know where to start."

"With the right help, you would." He indicated the armchairs either side of the occasional table, where tea tray still awaited attention. "Come. Let's enjoy some tea and talk about how it might go."

Cordelia served them both some tea, as she considered what he'd just said. The captain had more faith in her that she did herself. She'd never been taught how to manage her own affairs—neither had Lady Millicent come to that, nor really her grandfather. They'd relied on the attorney. Had that been wise?

"Thank you," the captain said, as she handed him a cup. "I think we each need something a little stronger after this afternoon's events, but this is very welcome for now. Tell me what you plan to do, give that your…companion can no longer manage the running of this household."

He must surely see the surprise on her face on being posed this question. She had expected him to instruct her what to do. It was the first time ever that she could recall being asked her opinion instead of being told what would happen. He held his cup wrapped in both hands, took an occasional sip of tea and waited, giving her time to think.

"Well…I suppose the first thing I should establish is the list of creditors to whom we owe money. And I could work out the total owed and see if the proceeds from the sale of the picture can cover them all. If not, I suppose I should settle with those whose bills go back furthest."

"All very logical and sensible. Are there other things you should try and find out?"

It was strange. Now she'd begun to think along these lines, the ideas were coming thick and fast.

"This house. I need to understand how my grandfather left things. I suppose I ought to go through the papers in his study. I know there was a will and something was set up for me for when I married, but even though it's been eight years since my betrothal I've not been told anything about the money—whether something should come to me if the marriage does not take place, which it seems is increasingly likely. The attorney should know. I shall need to make an appointment to speak with him as a matter of urgency. Mr Steadfast, he's called. I know that much."

"Do you trust him?"

"Why do you ask?"

"I would have thought, once you reached your age of majority, that any attorney worth his salt would have acknowledged the fact by confiding in you the kind of details you mention. As it is, it seems you have continued to be treated as a minor with no understanding of arrangements."

"Put like that, you know I'm not certain I do trust him."

"The last thing I want to do is interfere," the captain said, "but if you will kindly furnish me with some paper, I shall give you the name of a very trustworthy man. He was recommended to me by a friend and has recently acted for me most effectively and honestly. Given the seriousness of the questions you wish to put to this Steadfast character, it might help to have a reliable attorney beside you."

She opened the small bureau in the corner and found a pencil and sheet of paper and he stepped across to write out the details.

"Now I must take my leave," he told her. "I'll see Mr Christie arranges your payment before I leave Town."

"You're leaving?" The question was out before she could stop herself. He'd been so supportive. She felt she'd made a friend this afternoon and was a little bereft to think of him far away.

"A short visit to my family's estate in Wiltshire. I'm not sure how long I'll stay...but might I furnish you with that direction too? I'd very much like to know how you go on in these matters, if you have time to write, but more particularly how Lady Dunwoody fares."

"Of course," she said, automatically. He turned to add the address to the same paper, so missed the momentary look of panic on her face. How would she do it? She'd never written to a man before. One was not supposed to engage in such activities unless one was betrothed. The Marquess had sent a brief note following his departure eight years ago, but there had been no return address, so she'd never been able to reply and there had been no further word since.

"One more thing," the captain said, as he laid down the pencil. "Does Steadfast have access to Lady Dunwoody's bank account. I believe that's the one detailed on the auction papers."

"I don't know, but it would not surprise me. I wonder...could you ask Mr Christie to delay payment." She glanced at the sheet of paper with the attorney's details. "I think I might be advised to set up a new account in my own name. I'm sure Mr Fagg will tell me how that's to be done." She got to her feet. "Thank you so much, captain, for everything. I'm most grateful."

"I'm only too glad I was around. I'll see myself out. I hope Lady Millicent…well, I hope she's kept comfortable. I'll be sure to call and see how things are on my return."

He gave a bow and departed, leaving her feeling a strange mix of emotions. On the one hand she was so grateful for his purchasing the portrait, for rescuing her from those awful men and for being here to support her when she returned to this crisis with Lady Millicent. He'd also encouraged her to have the confidence to deal with this situation she now faced. It felt so daunting. Lady Millicent might be dying and while it might be possible to clear the most pressing debts with the proceeds of the auction, she had no further money coming in to maintain this house. How was she to cope? It was unlikely Uncle Harold would take pity on her, not after that scene between Lady Millicent and Aunt Florence.

6: Henry visits home

Henry had relished the cup of tea Cordelia had served him, not so much for the purpose of drinking it, but as a means of easing his aching right hand. He had cradled the cup in his palm and wrapped his left hand around the outside. The temporary warmth gave a little relief. It was many years since he'd engaged in a bare-knuckle encounter.

While he had fully intended to pay a visit to his parents' estate at some point during his leave, he had planned to spend a little longer in the capital first. Now he had good reason to bring the visit forward. He must deliver that portrait. Before departing, he had two tasks to complete. The first must be to visit James Fagg and forewarn him of Cordelia's probable approach, as well as deal with his own business in relation to the naval portrait, assuming Fagg's bid was successful. The second was to instruct Mr Christie not to pay the money from the sale of the portrait into the account detailed by Lady Dunwoody but to await instruction from Lady Cordelia.

There was a third task, which was easily achieved. By dint of a few well-placed questions in the vicinity of St James's Street he was able to establish the identity of the two drunken louts who had accosted Cordelia.

Back in Bond Street, Henry entered the hotel by the same route he'd left it. By gad, how much had happened in the few intervening hours! Up in his room he found a note had been pushed under the door. *Meet in the bar at seven*, it said. It was almost that now. The note was unsigned but he recognised Doc's hand. At least he knew it was not from Mrs Williams!

He rang for some hot water and freshened up, before donning clean linen and joining his friends downstairs. Both of them gave him an enquiring look, initially at his stylish outfit and then at his bruised hand. Word had evidently got round.

"Before you relate your adventures, Hal, the clerk wants an urgent word," Doc told him. "As soon as you came in, he said."

"We're mystified," Hutch added. "Wondered if they've possibly decided they cannot accommodate a navy thug who beats up Lord Farnham and Viscount Trumble!"

"Get me a brandy, will you?" Henry said, before making for the desk.

"Ah, Captain," the man greeted him. "Might you step through to the office?"

Henry wondered if the others were right, but the clerk's next words disabused him.

"The lady who accompanied you, captain. This is somewhat delicate. To put it in basic terms—she's gone. Must have packed her bag and left at some point this afternoon. No one witnessed her departure."

Henry knew exactly what was coming next.

"Thing is, it's a little sensitive. She failed to settle her bill."

Henry sighed. "Well, I'm very sorry. It's an awkward situation. The lady is not…" He paused there, thinking what was the point of denying responsibility? He'd introduced her into the hotel, after all. He sighed and met the man's quizzical gaze. "Add it to my own bill, but for heavens' sake don't mention her name in the invoice. As far as she's concerned you've written it off as a bad debt. Have it ready for Tuesday morning. I'll be departing then.

He re-joined his friends and was pleased to see the glass awaiting him. He downed it in one.

"Another?" Doc asked.

Henry nodded. "Then I'll be suitably fuelled to relate the events of my interesting day. Our hotel clerk's small administrative query was nothing compared to what else I've had to cope with.

"Well, well," said Doc, when he'd finished, "the poor young lady."

"Quite so. I believe her household is indeed very badly off," Henry said. "Things have come to such a pass that she's been driven to agreeing the sale of her fiancé's portrait."

"Which you purchased because it is actually not of the fiancé, but of your eldest brother—or leastways so you believe."

"I shall be taking it with me when I travel to Wiltshire on Tuesday. Godfrey will be able to confirm which artist he sat for some time in eighteen hundred and four. I was at sea by then, but I vaguely recall one of my mother's letters mentioning the finished item had never been delivered."

"You're travelling on Tuesday?" Hutch said. "You'll miss the Ascot Heath Races."

Henry shrugged. "Put a bet on for me. I could do with a replenishment of funds after my recent shopping expedition!"

"Did you get the other picture you wanted, by the famous naval artist?" Doc asked.

"Yes, I did, I'm pleased to say. Fagg handled things. He had to go quite high, but it was worth it. When else shall I find a picture of the *Europa* escorting the *Victory* to the battle lines of Trafalgar." That very precious canvas would be on its way, under guard, to his villa in Banstead by Monday, once Fagg had made the arrangements, but he did not share this piece of information with his friends, since he'd still not informed them he'd become a man of property.

"So, Hal, let me see if I've got this right?" Doc began. "You have spent much of today on furthering various causes of a certain young lady, who recently crashed out of a Bond Street shop into your arms and called you a clumsy oaf, or some such, for an incident that was entirely her own fault. Now we learn she's little right to be so hoity toity, being the possibly illegitimate daughter of a humble footman."

"That's hardly her fault," Hutch commented. "Besides, I seem to recall she's not a bad-looking wench, if she'd wipe that supercilious frown off her face."

Henry sighed. "I doubt we'll see her again in society, not with her chaperone at death's door. I get the impression she's never been taught even the basics of household management. The elderly lady did it all, or rather was guided in how to run things by the family attorney, who by all accounts has not managed things well at all. I've no time to get caught up in matters that are not my concern. However, I did suggest she approach another attorney to obtain impartial advice. It's up to her what she makes of it. Now, how about another round? Mine, I believe."

That was how he spoke of the situation to his friends, as if he would be having nothing further to do with Lady Cordelia Penshurst. Why then was she constantly in his thoughts? For the next day or two, he put it down to the fact that he'd been talking about her with James Fagg and with Mr Christie. Once he set off for Wiltshire, there were other matters to occupy him, but still she would come into his mind. How was the Lady Dunwoody? Had Cordelia managed to pay off the debts and keep the house? Had she sought the support of James Fagg? He supposed it was guilt. He'd departed that day with the self-righteous feeling that he'd done as much as he could to help her. On Monday, as planned, he'd made the visits to Fagg and Christie, but then he'd made an unscheduled third call, which had changed everything.

It had been as he'd driven back from visiting Fagg in Cheapside. His route had taken him along the Strand, where several of the London broadsheets had their offices. On impulse, he'd pulled up outside that of the *Morning Chronicle*, found a boy to watch his carriage and pair, and gone inside.

"Do you keep back copies of the newspaper?" he'd asked the clerk at the reception desk.

"Most of 'em," he'd been told. "What date had you in mind?"

So it was that he'd spent an hour or so systematically checking the issues for the summer of seventeen ninety-three, the period in which Cordelia had told him her parents had died. At last, he'd found what he sought. It was a brief paragraph headed *Tragic carriage accident.* It had been a bright August day and it was thought Mr Penshurst, who was driving, was dazzled by the sun and failed to take a turn in the lane, causing the carriage to overturn. It went on to report that he and his wife were mortally injured, but thankfully their five-year-old child was thrown clear and landed softly in a bush. The way Cordelia had related the incident, he'd had no idea she had been a passenger too.

That very first occasion on which Henry had seen her, he'd noticed her reluctance to climb into the hansom cab. Before she did so, she'd been on edge and irritable and quite rude to him, when she must have known she was responsible for crashing into him. He knew all too well that fear could make a person aggressive, rather than admit vulnerability. He'd seen it often enough in his crew. A few days ago, she'd walked the length of St James's Street, a notorious area for encountering young men with more money that manners, rather than hire a cab. It was no wonder her forehead was permanently creased in that frown. That five-year-old was still very much present, traumatised from the accident and no doubt confused and frightened by the changes that then took place in her life. Nevertheless, it might well do her good to take some control over her own destiny. He sensed that, in so many ways, she remained that dependent, obedient child who'd never been encouraged to grow up.

His departure for Wiltshire was well-timed. Were he still in Town, he had a strong feeling he might be tempted to call round daily at Berkeley Square for purposes other than communing with that dastardly parrot. As it was, he would no doubt be communing with his parents. His mother would describe all the female prospects for the marriage market this year. She had dropped more than a hint in recent letters that she'd like him to find a wife during this extended leave of his. His father, on the other hand, would quiz him about his career and just when he would progress from his own ship to commanding a fleet and ultimately become an admiral. His other brothers would be quoted as examples, one being a colonel and another a bishop. Only Godfrey was excused such ambition. Being the eldest, he would inherit the viscountcy and management of the estate in due course. The only cloud on the horizon, as far as the family was concerned, was future inheritance. Godfrey had wed more than ten years ago, but his wife had still not managed to produce a son, nor even a living child. Neither of the two middle brothers was married, hence the pressure on Henry to find a wife and have a family.

The situation had moved on since Henry had last been in touch. It was his mother who greeted him upon his arrival. His father was visiting a tenant on the far side of the estate, while the non-appearance of his brother and sister-in-law was soon explained.

"Oh Henry, your father's in despair. Dora had another miscarriage last week and the doctor has now told us there should be no further attempts or she may well die. Godfrey's sitting with her now. They're both very depressed about it."

"I'm very sorry." He knew what was coming next.

"Now I know this is not an appropriate time to be speaking of socialising in the county, but there is one rather beautiful young lady having her first season. Isabella is Lord Daneford's youngest. Not only that, she is due to have a friend visit for the summer, who's equally lovely, apparently. They were presented at the same time. She's still in Town but will be arriving in a few weeks. It's so much nicer socialising at country house-parties, much more intimate, rather than those awful jostling crowds in Town, where you can't hear yourself speak."

Henry understood his mother's unspoken message. If none of your elder brothers can produce an heir, it's your responsibility to do your duty—and as soon as possible. How she thought that ambition squared with having a life at sea for years at a time, in order to fulfil his father's wishes, Henry wasn't sure.

He did not encounter Godfrey until dinner time that evening and was quite shocked. He looked gaunt with worry and lack of sleep and, observing the little he ate, had also been losing weight and looked older than his thirty-eight years. The contrast with that relatively youthful portrait of eight years ago was painfully obvious. He doubted the poor man would want to be reminded of better times, but Henry had gone to considerable expense to obtain it and was determined to deliver it.

They were sharing a brandy in the billiards room, their parents having retired.

"I have a surprise for you and Dora," Henry told him. "At least I think I do—if the artist you posed for eight years ago was John Hoppner."

"It was! Don't tell me you've found it."

"I have." He told Godfrey how he'd happened to be at the auction when it came up.

"And is it properly finished? I read of a recent sale of incomplete works."

"Definitely—and an excellent image."

"So the artist was telling the truth. Father suspected he was fobbing us off because he'd got a student to finish it off and ruined it. It must have been stolen after all, as he claimed."

"I'll fetch it for you. It's in my room."

Later the next day, Henry gathered that even Dora had cheered up on seeing the missing portrait. She got her maid to help her dress and came down to supervise its hanging in the drawing room. "It's so nice to see you, Henry," she said. "Shall you be staying a while?"

Before he could respond, his mother spoke. "At least until the end of July, won't you, Henry?"

He shrugged and smiled ruefully at Dora. "The answer, apparently, is *yes*!" They all laughed. It had not been his intention to remain more than a couple of weeks, but given the circumstances, perhaps his support was owed. Besides, it would be a lot healthier to remain here rather than in Town, not least for the cleaner air. Were he to return to London, he risked further entanglement with Lady Cordelia Penshurst, word of which would be bound to reach his mother by dint of all her female society connections. And someone of Cordelia's background would be the last young lady to be approved as a marriage prospect. So, as the days turned into weeks and the various engagements planned for July loomed nearer, Henry reconciled himself to remaining in the country. He would have to endure his mother's match-making and try—however unsuccessfully—to avoid dwelling on Cordelia and how she might be faring.

The constancy of those wayward thoughts was proved towards the end of June, by his reaction to the receipt of a letter. His father handed it to him at luncheon.

"For you Henry. Looks like a lady's writing."

At those words, Henry's heart leapt within him, for it could surely only be from her. The other possibility was Mrs Williams, perhaps wishing to thank him for settling her hotel bill, but as he considered it, he thought it highly unlikely, since she knew neither of his generosity, nor that he'd come down to Wiltshire. His father passed him the letter and he studied for a neutral expression as he pocketed it, all the time aware of his mother's burning curiosity. He'd best say something.

"I expect it's from the old lady who sold Godfrey's portrait. I advised her on something and she promised to let me know how it went." That was almost the truth, after all. His mother's puzzled frown told him she did not believe him for a minute, for the firm style of the hand that had penned the direction was most certainly not that of an elderly lady!

It felt like an interminable time until he could escape and read it. He took it to the seclusion of the rose garden before breaking the seal.

To Captain Stanhope, Stanhope Hall, Wiltshire

Sir,

I trust your journey to the west country went smoothly and that your brother was pleased with his portrait. It must have been quite a surprise after all these years.

The proceeds of the sale met our accumulated debt almost exactly and it was such a relief to get matters straightened out. For that I have Mr Fagg to thank and I am so grateful that you put me in touch with him, for he has been most diligent in conducting various enquiries on my behalf. I showed him my grandfather's papers as well as records of various bonds and funds in the bank which have, for years, been under the control of Mr Steadfast. He found that the settlement my grandfather arranged for me is completely gone. According to Steadfast, it was paid out in gradual amounts to the Marquess of Dartington on the grounds of his betrothal to me. We cannot prove it, but it would not surprise me if a proportion was given to the attorney to keep him sweet. Mr Fagg does not think I can find recompense through the Court of Chancery, since the Marquess cannot be located. There were reports of someone fitting his description having perished in a skirmish in one of the South American countries, but we cannot be sure. He was not using the name Dartington by then.

You will no doubt wish to learn of Lady Dunwoody. She has done remarkably well and has got back some speech, although is still an invalid. She has constant nursing and is confined to her room, but can now be helped into a chair for part of the day. 'Scarlet' has been moved up there to give her company and she and Adèle are trying to teach it some manners!

As for me...you will note the change of address at the foot of this letter. Let me tell you how it came about. Having consulted Mr Fagg, it became clear I could not continue to reside in the Berkeley Square house with no money coming in, hence no ability to pay for staff, for Lady Millicent's nursing care, or for food and fuel, etcetera. I invited my uncle Harold, who has long wanted to acquire the use of his family's town house, to meet with me and Mr Fagg and we negotiated an arrangement beneficial to all parties. I agreed to move out, provided, when he moved in, he would take responsibility for Lady Dunwoody, who was his father's friend of many years, for the rest of her life. I am permitted to visit, provided I come in via the servants' entrance!

For my own part, I answered an advertisement in the paper to become chaperone and companion to an eighteen-year-old in her first season, hence I am residing in her father's very grand house in St James's Square. Given that I have never enjoyed a season myself, it is quite amusing, since the girl knows a good deal more of what is what than I do, although I am fast learning! I am kept very busy and that must be my excuse for not writing sooner. For the past week or so I have had not one, but two young ladies to supervise, since Felicity has a friend staying. At present we are busy packing, since we are to make a return visit to the friend's home in the country.

Well, I think that's about all my news. Thank you again for your support.

Yours sincerely, C Penshurst

June 26th 1812, Fanshawe House, St James's Square, Mayfair

The following day, Henry found an opportunity, when the talk at dinner turned to various families still in Town, to ask about the household in which Cordelia was currently residing.

"What of Fanshawe House, in St James's Square? Someone mentioned it was a very grand place."

"Oh, yes, very," his mother replied. "One wonders how long Baronet Fanshawe will hold on to it, given his life-style. The poor daughter was left motherless when she was quite young. But a wealthy great aunt, who knew the Baronet's predilections all too well, settled a fortune on her—more than thirty thousand pounds, we're told. She gets it when she's twenty-one, or her husband does when she weds. I imagine she will be a leading catch of the season. The baronet, no doubt, would like her to snare an amenable husband as soon as maybe—one who might be sensitive to his new father-in-law's needs and keep him in funds!"

"Humph," grunted Henry's father. "More like keep the bookies and owners of the gambling hell holes happy."

"She's said to be a lovely girl," his mother continued. "In fact, you'll see for yourself. She's the friend due to visit Isabella Daneford next month, so you're bound to meet her. Lord Daneford would make the better father-in-law, of course."

It took Henry a moment or two to work through the logic. If the Fanshawe heiress was being chaperoned for the summer by Cordelia Penshurst and Miss Fanshawe was visiting her friend in Wiltshire and Henry was to attend the same county events, then it must follow, as night followed day, that he would soon encounter Cordelia again. He would like to have replied to her letter at once, but it was more than likely she would have quit Town before it could arrive. He would see her soon enough, a happy thought indeed, though why it should be, he couldn't quite fathom.

7: The London season

June 1812, Mayfair, London

How very strange life could be, Cordelia thought, as she emerged from sleep and gazed up at the brocade drapes fastened with gold plaited ropes against the bed posts. It was rather like stepping onto the front of the stage as the curtains were opened. Her role now certainly felt like a performance. A month ago, she had been a timid victim of circumstances. Now, by the eve of mid-summer's day, she had developed the stature of all the other matrons who escorted young debutantes to high society gatherings during their first season and at least some of the confidence required for the role.

She had also been allocated this apartment, fitted out with elegant Sheraton cabinets, tables and chairs, with expensive brocade curtains in a striking Jacobean flower design on a blue background and a matching Axminster rug, which filled the space between the bed and the fireplace. She even had her own washroom attached. The walls were crowded with old family portraits and she guessed this room might have once belonged to the mistress of the house. But there had been no mistress for many years and it was Cordelia who was now to supervise the entry of the young Felicity Fanshawe into society.

This new direction in her life had been forced upon her by circumstances. It had been a revelation to work through her grandfather's papers with the knowledgeable and patient Mr Fagg. Business matters were, in fact, quite easy to understand when they were clearly explained.

She'd even stood up to Uncle Harold in the matter of Lady Millicent's care. She'd never have had the courage without Mr Fagg by her side, and no doubt her uncle's reaction would have been less accommodating without the attorney's presence. Uncle Harold had not liked it one bit when she had pointed out how he and his brothers had let down their aging father by not supervising the activities of Mr

Steadfast. Now the poor old lady, who'd tried to cope since their father's death, was owed some recompense and some compassion. As for herself, she had reminded him, Steadfast's mishandling of her grandfather's affairs had brought about her own current plight—she must now work for a living, since their neglect had resulted in the portion her grandfather had intended for her being given away. How he allocated responsibility for that situation was between him and his conscience. She told him she would not take matters further provided he agreed to take care of Lady Millicent. Mr Fagg had already warned her a legal challenge would take an inordinately long time and was unlikely to succeed anyway, so her threat was an idle one, but evidently Uncle Harold was not aware of the fact.

Cordelia endeavoured to visit Lady Millicent at least two or three times a week, when she could. But she had new responsibilities and very little time off.

Felicity Fanshawe was a lively girl, only recently turned eighteen. She was not an outstanding beauty but, with her rosebud mouth, lively blue eyes and blonde curls, was pretty enough. Looks were not the only currency here, for Cordelia had gleaned from household gossip that she came with a huge inheritance. The girl would be courted and flattered by all the gentlemen and Cordelia saw her own function as instilling some awareness and common sense into the girl's head.

Cordelia had begun this challenge during her first week in post, when she'd sat Felicity down to plan their activities for the rest of June. Cordelia had never had cause to keep anything resembling an appointment book, but she did so now. Where they came from, Cordelia knew not, given she'd never been through a season herself, but she found various nuggets of advice pouring from her lips in relation to the calendar of social events published in the paper and the pile of invitation cards that had begun to accumulate ever since Felicity's official presentation in April. On that occasion, she'd been chaperoned by the elderly lady, who'd been the girl's companion since the death of her mother. Unfortunately, shortly after that significant event, the old lady, who'd suffered for some time with a weak heart, had passed away. There had followed a brief period of mourning, which had resulted in Felicity missing half the season. Since Cordelia's appointment as her new companion and chaperone, the girl was tumbling over herself to attend everything she could. Cordelia simply brought some common sense to bear on the process.

"Let's look at what's coming up and plan our commitments," Cordelia had told the girl. "If you attend every event to which you've been invited, you'll be so short of rest, you'll likely fall asleep at the supper table and those pretty eyes of yours will have dark circles around them."

Thus it was that Cordelia imposed some structure and sense of priorities on the girl's outings into society. "We will choose only two balls per week and ensure we have no commitments on the following day," Cordelia insisted. "Thus you will be in to receive callers the next morning and able to accept carriage rides in the afternoon and rest in the evening. In between those occasions we shall attend a ladies' morning party or afternoon tea. That is where you will demonstrate to the doting mamas of all those young gentlemen who've been courting you, that you can hold a sensible conversation about more than the latest fashions or who was on your dance card at the last ball you attended."

"Isabella won't like it, when she comes," Cordelia was tritely information. "She likes to go to everything."

Now the dreaded Isabella had arrived and Cordelia was due to escort her and Felicity to the coming evening's chosen event, which Cordelia anticipated with less than enthusiasm. There were a number of reasons for this. Chief among them was the question of how she was to supervise the activities of two rather wilful young ladies instead of one. It would be different if they were quiet, biddable girls, but that was untrue of either of them. Felicity, in Cordelia's opinion, was prone to wear her heart on her sleeve. The young man she'd danced with for two sets at Mrs Dawson's grand ball last week had been left in no doubt how his young partner felt about him. She couldn't take her eyes off him for the rest of the evening, constantly fluttering her eyelids his way, not concentrating on her steps so she trod on her current partner's toes more than once. She then spent the journey back to St James's Square reciting to Cordelia a list of all the other events he'd informed her he would be attending.

Of the two girls, Cordelia anticipated Felicity's friend might be even more challenging to manage. While Felicity might be considered pretty, Isabella was beautiful, a striking girl with rich chestnut hair, wide-spaced hazel eyes and well-defined cheek bones above a full-lipped mouth and well-endowed in that place men were attracted to. She did not require the kind of padding and pushing that some young ladies employed to enhance their bust.

Another drawback of this evening's event concerned where it was. The Marchioness of Hertford resided in Manchester Square, which required them to drive the whole distance across Mayfair from south to north. It was the self-same journey they had made to Mrs Dawson's house only last week and involved far longer in a carriage than was comfortable for Cordelia, particularly with the considerable number of crossroads to be negotiated. She was quite dreading the journey they would later be making to Wiltshire.

Her thoughts were interrupted by a tap on the door from the maid delivering her morning tray. She was a cheerful girl and, as she drew back the curtains to let in the sunshine, she chatted in her usual way.

"The young ladies are still asleep, my lady," Cordelia was informed. "Methinks they were gossiping together well into the early hours."

"I see. Let them sleep for now. Perhaps take them some refreshments around noon. I expect they'll be wanting most of the afternoon to prepare for tonight."

"Yes, my lady," the girl said, before leaving the room.

Good, thought Cordelia, I shall linger for another half hour at least.

There was very little for Cordelia to do in preparation for the evening outing, short of dress herself. Isabella had brought her personal maid with her and was sharing her with Felicity. So Cordelia ordered her bath filled and enjoyed a leisurely bathe before selecting her gown for the evening. Being a mere chaperone meant she did not require the latest fashionable design. In fact, she'd decided it was far more preferable to wear something old-fashioned and in as pale a colour as possible, so as to blend into the background and avoid drawing attention to herself.

She selected her best evening gown, which she'd acquired from a useful shop in Regent Street, which retailed out-of-date fashions at reasonable prices and included the cost of a few simple alterations, where required. This gown was from at least six years ago, in white muslin, naturally, with a high neck and long sleeves and a lace trim around the hem. She did her hair in its usual plait wound on top of her head and arranged Lady Millicent's silk rose to one side. It was too warm to bother with a pelisse or a mantle and she didn't possess one of those newly fashionable Spencer jackets.

She'd arranged with Baronet Fanshawe's carriage driver to be ready to set off at nine-thirty to be in good time for the doors opening at ten. Of the baronet himself there was no sign. He'd attended the Bath races earlier in the week and was evidently not yet back. The friend he'd accompanied had provided the transport, so his own carriage had been left at Cordelia's disposal.

He was a dissipated man, who had little time for his daughter and none at all for her chaperone. She was simply a servant in his eyes and he had barely spoken two words to her since her arrival. The fact of his not requiring his carriage was convenient as far as his daughter's social engagements were concerned, but Cordelia soon gathered that his generosity was not entirely due to consideration for his daughter's needs. Rather, as the household's gossip soon informed Cordelia, it was the consequence of deliberate choice. He made little use of it for any distance in order to avoid the cost of tolls or changes of horse, which he could ill afford.

As regards her management of the two young ladies under her supervision, Cordelia had what she realised was probably a somewhat unusual approach. Where many chaperones would be laying down the law, Cordelia was rather feeling her way into the role and thus far had allowed Felicity a good deal of leeway in regard to selecting the events she wished to attend, within the limits set by Cordelia. She'd also allowed her to decide for herself what to wear at each occasion.

Thus, when the two young ladies descended the stairs ready to depart, Cordelia was seeing their selected outfits for the first time, except she couldn't, given that they each wore the newest style of long mantle made of fine kerseymere on top of their gowns. Felicity's was in a blue that matched her eyes and, from what Cordelia could see beneath it, also matched the gown's skirt. Isabella's was in maroon, toning nicely with the deep rose of her skirt. Isabella's maid had done a fine job with their hair, both being fixed up and entwined with ribbons to match their respective dresses.

She would not get a proper view of the dresses beneath their mantles until they arrived at their destination, if they ever did, and handed in their cloaks. It was Isabella who first drew their attention to the other traffic crowding the streets.

"We are going extraordinarily slowly," Isabella commented. "Is it always so crowded in Town?"

Felicity pulled aside one of the window curtains. It was still light enough to make out the scene. "There are carriages in all directions," she said. "Some are not moving at all and the horses are getting quite restless."

Cordelia was quite happy with the situation, although she could not admit as much to her companions. Going at a slower pace meant they were less likely to crash and being delayed in arriving meant they would spend less time at the party. They finally descended from their carriage a little after eleven and, as they joined the dense crowd trying to gain admittance to the grand mansion that was Hertford House, Cordelia glanced about them. There were still carriages nose to tail along the route they had taken from Oxford Street, but similar hold-ups applied along Portman Square to the west and Welbeck Street to the east. It appeared the entire population of London was trying to gain admittance and as a consequence had brought the capital's traffic to a complete standstill!

When, at last, the three of them mounted the front steps and passed under the colonnaded portico, Cordelia realised what a foolish choice it had been on Felicity's part to insist on attending tonight. It had been portrayed as an *assembly*. This, it transpired, was an opportunity to wander around the huge principal rooms on the ground floor of Hertford House, admire the sophisticated decorations, refresh oneself with tasty ices, fruits and confectionary—if one could get anywhere near the refreshment table— and hold erudite conversations on topics of interest.

Felicity had chosen it for the status it carried. The Marchioness of Hertford held three or four such gatherings each season and they were the top of the tree as regards status. Guests were said to include the Prince of Wales and other royals, foreign ambassadors and a generous representation of the nobility. However, the girl had not understood the significance of the word *assembly*. She did now, as did her friend. They were squashed in amongst the crowd that quite filled the entrance lobby, a large enough hall in normal times, but not when hundreds of guests were trying to gain admittance at the same time.

"It's such a squash," Isabella complained. "My skirts are being quite crushed."

"It's impossible," Felicity added. "How is anyone to form a dance set when there's no floor space?"

They were having to shout to make themselves heard above the constant buzz of other conversations and an elderly lady beside them soon put them right.

"Oh, there's no dancing," she told them. "I certainly wouldn't have come along for that. No, it's more like one of those conversaziones, where conversation is the order of the day. There are some wonderful displays. One room is even formed into a Turkish tent panelled with looking glasses and decorated with flowers and shrubs."

Their informant was soon swept away by the general thrust of the crowd still trying to gain admittance. Cordelia decided she'd had enough.

"Girls, do not bother to remove your cloaks. I doubt we'd ever locate them again. If I have to stay in here much longer, I shall pass out with the heat and lack of air. Come."

They didn't argue as she led them painstakingly across to the side of the hall where a footman stood waiting to relieve guests of coats and hats. He was doing very little business.

"I need to get my wards to some fresh air," she told the man. "May we exit through the kitchens? It's impossible at the front door."

"Of course, ma'am," he said. He sounded pleased to have something useful to do. "This way."

"And we need to locate our carriage," she told him, as they followed him down the service stairs to the basement rooms. "It's the Fanshawe crest, a dark red chaise with a pair of bay horses."

"Of course, my lady. If you'd like to wait by the scullery door here. I doubt he'll have gone far."

Cordelia saw the look he was giving Isabella, who was fluttering her eyelashes and pretending not to notice. It made her rather wonder at her mother's romance with her footman father.

Cordelia was delighted to escape back to the house before midnight. The return ride had been quiet, not only due to the relative lack of traffic going in their direction, but also due to the silence of the two girls. Isabella was sulking, while Felicity was embarrassed at selecting an event that was clearly designed for the older members of the *haut ton* rather than young bucks seeking marriage prospects from amongst recently presented young ladies.

"Why didn't you warn me?" Felicity asked Cordelia, with a pout and a frown, as they at last entered Fanshawe House.

"I didn't know any more that you did," Cordelia replied. "Let us put it down to experience and learn to plan our social calendar with more circumspection in future. Tomorrow, perhaps you'd both like to join me at breakfast before we all attend St George's for morning worship. Then in the afternoon we can review your various invitations and discuss what we'd like to do in the coming week. Could you manage ten o'clock do you think? Goodnight to you both." She averted her face as she climbed the stairs to avoid them seeing her smile.

The following morning, Cordelia was quite surprised to find the two girls already seated in the breakfast room. What was less unexpected was the protests about attending church.

"Come now, girls, do you not think your future husbands will be impressed at your commitment to our Saviour? And, naturally, they will generally be in company with their mothers."

They evidently saw the possibilities in this and there were no further objections.

Throughout her forays into society with Felicity, Cordelia had been constantly aware of the possibility of encountering those two so-called gentlemen who'd accosted her in St James's Street. Thus far, it had not happened and morning worship at the society church was the very last venue she expected to meet them. As they left the service, Cordelia led the two girls through the main door and her heart sank as she spotted them, standing at the top of the steps apparently conversing. Neither of them recognised her, dressed as she was in her best silk pelisse, but she could tell they'd not actually looked at her properly. Their interest lay elsewhere. Had they been lying in wait? Then she heard Felicity's light giggle and turned in time to see the two cads rising from the bows they'd made, their top hats in their hands. Cordelia kept moving and the girls had no choice but to follow, but she gave a surreptitious glance over her shoulder and saw both girls doing the same towards their admirers. Damn! Cordelia would have to trust they did not encounter them at any further events before their departure to Isabella's home in the west country, which, so far as she was concerned, could not come soon enough.

8: A change of direction

June 1812, Stanhope Hall, Wiltshire

Henry was struck by how quickly this past month at the family estate had gone and, more unexpectedly, how much he'd enjoyed it. Being back in the bosom of family was perhaps a trite and sentimental way to describe it, but it had been relaxing and fulfilling to reconnect with his parents and Godfrey and get to know his sister-in-law Dora. His other two brothers had also found time to visit, making it the first occasion for ten years when they'd all been under this roof together. Their visit had coincided with the middle period of June, when there had been perfect conditions for hay-making and they had all made an attempt to revive their skills with a scythe, learnt many years before.

On other days, he and Godfrey had ridden out together, by turns covering all corners of the large estate and visiting each of the tenants at least once. They did the same on the afternoon following Henry's receipt of that letter, on which topic he'd been surprised to receive no more than a quizzical look from his mother. He was soon to discover that she'd appointed her eldest son as chief investigator. It was when he and Godfrey had ridden to a high-up view-point at the north end of the estate. They dismounted and left the horses happily grazing while they relaxed at the top of the grassy slope that had once been a boyhood haunt for rolling down like a barrel or, in rare snowy winters, tobogganing.

"So who is she, my secretive brother?"

They both knew what he meant, but Henry decided to play coy. "To whom are you referring?"

"You know very well! The writer of that letter you were so self-conscious about receiving. It was no more from an elderly lady than I'm a Dutchman."

"She was writing on *behalf* of the elderly lady I mentioned," he responded. "Nothing to get excited about."

Godfrey's eyes narrowed. He clearly did not believe Henry for a minute.

"Well, I wish you joy, whether you take one of Mama's choices or your own. I'm afraid there are expectations, Hal."

Henry gave him a rueful smile and nodded. "A fact I'd have had to be blind to miss."

"The thing is, old chap, there's something I need to tell you."

Henry wondered for a moment whether this was some dreadful news about more than Dora's health, but the tremulous quiver in his brother's voice sounded more like excitement than fear.

"What is it?" he asked.

"Dora and I are moving abroad."

"You're what! In the middle of a war?"

"We're going to Madeira, which is quite safe, the Portuguese being allies and the British in, you might say, friendly occupation at present. I've purchased a small hotel, which we intend to run as a centre for convalescence. They'll be plenty of customers, both military and civilian. The climate will do Dora so much good and she'll relish the fruit and vegetables she'll be able to cultivate."

Henry's mind was working with quick logic and he saw at once where this was going.

"Father knows?"

"We discussed it last week. They both think it a sensible step, not least for Dora's health. She's been through a hell of a time. But…"

He hesitated there and Henry completed the sentence for him.

"What about the future of the estate?"

Godfrey nodded. "Quite. He wants to sign it over to you in due course, and also make you the one to inherit the title of course. They're both very keen for you to take a wife and produce an heir or two."

"No Admiral Stanhope then?"

Godfrey gave a wry smile. "We had one of those a few generations back, I believe. Besides, you've given the service ten years of your life."

Henry sighed. "I might feel more amenable were things at a different stage. Now Lord Liverpool's taken over as prime minister, he's fully committed to pursuing the war until Napoleon is defeated. Wellington's making a difference in the Peninsular, but we've a way to go. On top of that we're now at war with the United States and a naval presence will be needed in the Atlantic more than ever."

Godfrey tried another tack. "You've enjoyed these past few weeks here, that's obvious."

Henry shrugged. "Of course. It's a lovely place at this time of year." He didn't add that he now understood Godfrey's plan of campaign. During Henry's stay, they'd visited every inch of the estate and every person who relied on it for their living, a not-so-subtle form of emotional blackmail.

Henry got to his feet and stood, arms akimbo, looking down at his brother. Madeira would do Godfrey good too, bring more colour to his cheeks and put some more healthy flesh on his bones. Not only that, he'd be giving up so much himself. He'd been reared to take over from their father.

"Look, this is all rather sudden," Henry said. "I need some time to think things through. Would you mind if I go for a solo ride? I'll be back by sundown."

Godfrey scrambled to his feet too and stretched out a hand and shook his warmly. "Of course. As long as you don't gallop hell-for-leather to Portsmouth and embark on the first available vessel. See you later."

The first thing Henry did after mounting was indeed to gallop. He went the entire length of the ridge that formed the estate's northern boundary. That meant concentrating on the ground before him to avoid tussocks and rabbit holes. At last, when the horse was frothing at the mouth and he was panting hard, he slowed the big stallion to a walk and patted him on the neck.

"I think that did us both good," he told the creature. It was gratifying to find he retained the seat he'd developed in his youth, for he hardly ever rode these days. And that was it, really. He'd lived here, aside from periods away at school, until he'd turned eighteen. How easy it would be to slot back into the privileged life-style, the large house, the fresh produce, the healthy air, the satisfaction of holding an entire community's wellbeing within one's remit. His father loved it, he knew, and had never known anything else. His mother had played her part, not only producing four sons, but taking to managing a houseful of servants very readily, a role she'd in turn been born and trained up to.

If he agreed to this drastic alteration in his priorities, there would be expectations. The most important would be for him to marry and produce progeny, preferably male. His mother would push for him to choose someone from the same background. She clearly already had Isabella Daneford in mind, although her friend Felicity Fanshawe with her thirty thousand pounds would probably pass muster too! One thing was clear. She could not be someone with a questionable social background like Cordelia Penshurst. Yet there was something about that vulnerable young woman that drew him. Why else had he found himself thinking about her so much? Why had he experienced that physical tug of pleasure inside him on receiving her letter.

The answer was probably to do with the fact that she had somehow transformed herself from a victim of circumstances to a bold woman making her own way in the world. He could not but admire her for that. He also liked to think that the way he had encouraged her to have faith in her natural abilities, together with the practical step of putting her in touch with a trustworthy attorney, had not a little to do with her discovering, within herself, the power to determine her own life. He sensed that she would do just fine, even if she never married or had a family, and he was pleased to have contributed to her successful launch into the world as a competent, independent adult, riding stormy seas as well as calm.

That thinking brought him back to the decision he must make. By the time he clopped across the stable yard and delivered his tired mount to a stable hand, he'd come to a decision. He went to his room to wash and change and sent a servant with a message for his father, requesting a conference before dinner. The message came back that he would await Henry in the library. That brought memories of his wayward, younger self. He had ever been summoned to this room for a telling-off. The punishment generally fitted the crime and cook was forever receiving his assistance with scrubbing the baking tins for stealing a cake from the kitchens without permission. His father didn't believe in beatings. Henry was aware that attitude was the same one he'd carried with him to his own shipboard command, and was not a little to do with the fact that he'd gathered a fine crew about him on the *Europa*. The men appreciated a fair and humane captain and he was never short of hands wanting to serve aboard her.

His father greeted Henry with raised eyebrows and held out a glass of whisky, already poured and waiting for him.

"I take it Godfrey's spoken with you?" he said, raising his own glass. "Your health."

"And yours," Henry responded, keeping his glass aloft as he added, "And Godfrey and Dora's too. It's a sensible move they plan to make."

"It puts you in a difficult position. I recognise that."

"Not so much difficult, as unexpected," Henry said. "There's no question as to my choice. There is no other option. The estate must go on."

He could see the relief on his father's face. The tension that had been there quite melted away and he smiled.

"You're sure."

Henry nodded. "As a priority, I shall have to make for London and speak with the naval office at Somerset House. Given that I've done ten years, I can't foresee a problem in resigning."

"They'll understand," his father said. "They're all gentlemen, after all. If necessary, I can have a word in the right quarters."

That was the way things were done, Henry thought, cynically. He was now set on a somewhat altered course to become one of the privileged elite as a viscount instead of an admiral!

"I suggest we delay informing my mother until the paperwork is satisfactorily concluded," Henry said. "I don't anticipate a problem, but just in case. Meanwhile, I'll have a quiet word with Godfrey, to reassure him."

"Sensible decision," his father said. "Your mother will have the match-making done and the banns called before you can say Jack Robinson. Shall you drive yourself to Town in your curricle?"

He shook his head. "Best take the post for speed. With luck, I'll be able to see someone on Monday."

On reaching Town, Henry made directly for Somerset House and his business was concluded by Monday afternoon, whereupon he headed for Steven's Hotel in hopes of a room for the night, before making the return journey to Wiltshire on Tuesday. Naturally, the clerk remembered him, after all the embarrassment with Mrs Williams.

"Of course, captain," the man said. "I can find you a room. And your friend, Mr Garvey, is still here. He's out at present but will be back here before an evening engagement, he told me."

"Excellent, I might join him," Henry said, privately thinking it rather depended on what the chosen activity might be. "Perhaps I could leave him a note. I shall be out myself for a couple of hours."

Henry had not exactly planned it, and he could hardly call at the house in St James's Square, where Cordelia now resided. However, there was no reason he could not pay a courtesy call upon Lady Dunwoody.

On arrival, he was conducted into the familiar drawing room by a butler. Evidently the household now had a full complement of staff and, despite asking for Lady Dunwoody, it was apparently necessary to be vetted by the mistress first, for the lady who stood and stepped forward to greet him was Harold's wife, the woman who'd had that altercation with Lady Dunwoody. He gave a bow, which took in the other woman, who remained seated. She had the same round face and greying hair and blue eyes. They must surely be sisters. They looked equally confused at the arrival of this stranger.

"Lady Elderfold, pardon me for disturbing your afternoon unannounced," he said. "I had hoped to pay my compliments to Lady Dunwoody."

"Oh, I see," the woman said, her voice carrying a sharp timbre of something—disapprobation perhaps. "She's confined to her room these days. I'll have you taken up." She nodded at the maid standing silently in the corner and the girl went to pull the bell.

The butler soon appeared and led Henry upstairs and along the corridor to the back of the house, where he proceeded to tap the lady's bedroom door. A familiar figure appeared and Henry acknowledged her with a bow.

"Adèle, bonjour. Est-ce que votre Maîtresse reçoit des visiteurs aujourd'hui ?"

"Mais oui," she said, giving him a broad smile and ushering him in, while the butler, looking a little surprised, retreated back whence he'd come.

"Hello captain," a frail voice spoke from the chair near the fireplace, where a modest fire burned. "What a lovely surprise!" The lasting effect of the apoplexy was evident in the droop of her mouth on one side and it affected her ability to form words. She spoke quite slowly and with evident effort.

"My lady," Henry greeted her with a bow. "I hope you don't mind my calling like this. I unexpectedly found myself in Town and thought you might like to know how delighted my brother was to receive his portrait at last."

"Good. Cordelia explained the story. That dastardly Dart turned out to be a thief as well as a deceiver."

"It's good to find you able to leave your bed, my lady."

"But boring. May I offer you some tea. It's so pleasant to have company, other than my friend *Scarlet* over there."

Henry glanced round at the corner behind him and observed the bundle of red feathers apparently asleep on his perch. But on hearing his name, he promptly came to life and danced about a bit, before repeating, "Hello captain."

"Cover him over, Adèle," she instructed, "before he says anything less tasteful. I miss Cordelia. She visits when she can, but they keep her very busy. Of course, short of allowing me bed and board, Harold and Florence have nothing much to do with me."

Henry had no idea if the lady was aware of Cordelia writing to him, so decided not to mention it. Their conversation continued through tea on safe topics such as the weather and the price of coal and how long he would be in Town. He did not mention the life-changing decision he'd recently come to—although it would soon be published in the *Gazette*—while she made no further mention of Cordelia. Adèle stayed the entire time and had to help her mistress sip from her cup.

Henry took his leave as soon as politeness would allow. It was so damnably hot in the room and convention would not permit him to remove his jacket. He wondered whether he should leave a message for Cordelia, but, before he could form the words, Lady Dunwoody forestalled him.

"I'll tell Cordelia you called."

"Yes. Please convey my good wishes."

Back at the hotel, he found Doc returned and joined him in the bar.

"Nice to have your company," Doc said. "I've grown somewhat bored with my own."

"Only a fleeting visit," Henry told him. "I'm travelling back tomorrow."

"Well, you may as well enjoy yourself while you're here. I was planning on another visit to the Vauxhall Gardens this evening. There's one of those regular firework displays and concerts, not to mention shady walkways in which to get lost with wayward young ladies."

"I see," Henry said, putting on a schoolmasterly frown. "I had perhaps better accompany you as chaperone, in that case, but I've not brought anything formal with me to wear."

"Won't your navy uniform do?"

"Ah…there's something I need to tell you."

Henry's revelation led to a good deal of soul-searching by his colleague. At thirty-five, Doc had served on several ships and had seen more battles than Henry. He was not that surprised at what the man told him.

"That makes a certain decision for me," he told Henry. "I've been offered a position at St Thomas' Hospital as a surgeon, but also to lecture in anatomy and surgery. It's time I settled down anyway. The alternative has somewhat lost its appeal these days."

"When do you begin, if you accept the post?"

"September."

"In that case, would you like to accompany me to Wiltshire in the interim? I shall invite my mother to act on your behalf. Then perhaps she'll spend less time nagging me about finding a wife."

"I'd like nothing better. It appears I shall make a more enthusiastic subject for her matchmaking than you will!"

So, in cheerful mood, they set off for Vauxhall Gardens, timing their arrival for eight. As they paid their four shillings and passed through the gate, Doc explained that this was the best time to arrive, for there would be crowds of people all settling into their seats for the concert. He knew the best place to sit in order to peruse the young ladies in the audience and identify those worth pursuing. Once the concert ended, it was simply a matter of following the same paths and contriving an introduction.

The band struck up with God Save the King and the chatter amongst the audience hushed. By the time everyone had settled back in their seats, Doc had selected his quarry.

"See that girl in the red dress, in one of the middle rows over there," Doc whispered in his ear. "She's not interested in the music, see. She's looking about her for something and I doubt it's her sister. She's husband hunting."

"Aren't they all at that age?" Henry replied. "She looks quite young."

"All to the good, my friend," Doc said. You can teach 'em how to please you in bed and they're young enough to have plenty of stamina in that regard."

Henry observed the young woman's gaze sweeping around the other occupants of the tiered seating. She reached them, staring particularly at Doc, who raised his hat and gave a slight bow in her direction. Her reaction was interesting. Instead of blushing, fluttering her eyelids and looking away, she continued gazing boldly in his direction, tipping her head in a way that seemed to say *I'm interested, but what have you got to offer.*

"She's game," Doc said. "That red dress says it all."

Only at that moment did Henry allow his own gaze to examine the girl's party, as she turned to whisper something to the girl beside her.

Surely, they had a chaperone. Then he recognised her, seated on the other side of the flirtatious girl in the red dress. It was Cordelia!

9: Pursued

Monday 29th June 1812, Vauxhall Gardens, London

As far as Cordelia was concerned, the quicker she got her two charges to Wiltshire, the better. Today would be their last engagement in Town. Tomorrow would be spent packing their trunks and they would travel on Wednesday in grand style, for Isabella's father was sending his carriage for them.

Cordelia had known from the moment she first encountered Lady Isabella Daneford that she was used to going her own way. This trait demonstrated itself in various ways, such as voicing decided opinions on everything from which events they should attend to passing personal, often derogatory, remarks about the various hostesses who had the dubious honour of welcoming them through their portals. These were not always delivered in the kind of whisper she had a moment ago demonstrated to her friend, as she leant across Cordelia to share some secret she did not wish Cordelia to overhear. They had taken their seats in Vauxhall Gardens ready for the concert and Cordelia sighed with relief. The end of this venture into high society was near. It would be so much easier once they reached Isabella's home, where her sole responsibility would be Felicity.

She thought back over the past couple of weeks of this double load of supervision. The most glaring example of Isabella's independent spirit, and the one that gave Cordelia the most discomfort, was her choice of dress. Evidently her mother had no influence, or possibly it was from her mother that Isabella had inherited her flamboyance. The personal maid she'd brought with her was not much help. She seemed to be running her own campaign to get her mistress to expose as much naked flesh as possible, or perhaps she had no authority to prevent it.

Unbeknownst to Isabella or Felicity, Cordelia had overheard enough of the two girls' shared confidences to cause her concern, but she kept her counsel and said nothing. Were she to reveal how she had come to eavesdrop they would thereafter be far more careful and she would learn nothing at all.

The weather throughout most of June had been warm and sunny and, on afternoons when they were not out, the two young ladies had developed the habit of making use of the garden of Fanshawe House. It was a substantial one, but their favourite spot was in one corner, where the so-called garden seat stood, which they evidently believed gave them some privacy. It was in effect a small open-sided building with its own roof. There were actually two seats, consisting of a long bench on each side of a central dividing wall, beneath a portico held up by tall columns on each corner. It was constructed entirely of stone in the same Palladian style as the house.

On this particular occasion, the Saturday before their planned departure, Cordelia had gone into the garden to pick a few flowers to take to Lady Dunwoody later in the afternoon, being the only opportunity to visit before they left Town. She happened to be on the far side of the seat when the girls took possession of their usual bench facing the ornamental garden and were immediately in earnest conversation. Cordelia did not approve of eavesdropping, but in this instance she'd already heard sufficient to think she ought to. If she showed herself now, the girls would be mortified at learning she'd heard every word.

"How do you know all those things about…men, Isabella?" she heard Felicity ask. "Did your mother tell you?"

"Poo to that," Isabella replied. "I have three older sisters wed. I made them tell me. I knew what they got up to before the vows were spoken and they didn't want our father to know." So the little vixen was not averse to engaging in some blackmail when it suited her. What a little manipulator, thought Cordelia.

"So, what *did* they get up to?" she heard Felicity ask, in a tremulous tone that rather implied she didn't really want to know the answer.

"Kissing, naturally, on the lips. But they also touched each other in certain intimate places—I mean *underneath* their clothing—at least the two younger ones did. I don't know about the eldest. She married someone much older and from what the other two have told me, she doesn't much enjoy the…er…bedroom."

"So, when they do…that thing to you, does it hurt? I've seen those marble statues in the hall in your father's house. Their…thing doesn't look big enough to do any harm at all."

"Oh, Felicity, you don't know anything, do you?"

Cordelia was quite glad to hear Felicity's retort to her superior friend. It was refreshing to hear her speak up for herself, but her answer also confirmed her relative innocence.

"As you know, I don't have any sisters, nor a mother and I don't think my father is going to sit me down and explain."

"What about your chaperone? On second thoughts, I doubt she'll be any help. She wouldn't say boo to a goose and, as for her dress-sense, it's non-existent. I doubt she'll ever catch a man."

That was probably true enough, thought Cordelia. She did wonder just how experienced Felicity was with the opposite sex. Was she speaking theoretically or had she already sampled a man's intimate touches, or worse?

The topic of conversation had then switched to discussing the latest fashions and, as she listened, Cordelia had yet more cause for concern. She even wondered if she ought to find a reason for them not to attend the Vauxhall Gardens on Monday evening.

"My new dress has arrived," Isabella said. "It's so daring, I can't tell you. The style has only come into vogue this month so hardly anyone will have a gown like mine yet. It goes daringly low in the front with a V in the middle and goes down a little at the sides too."

"Goodness," exclaimed Felicity, "it must reveal half your bosom!"

"At least," Isabella said. "And the back is lower too. I shall wear an Indian shawl around my shoulders until we get there, just for modesty. And the colour. It's the most wonderful scarlet. Would you like to come and see?"

Cordelia had waited a few minutes after their departure before gathering up her somewhat wilted bunch of flowers and making for the scullery to place them in water. She was surprised Isabella knew the word modesty!

At least she had been prepared for the sight of the girl this evening, when they set off in the Fanshawe carriage for Vauxhall Gardens. By contrast to her friend, Felicity had on a pale blue silk gown with traditional lace trim and looked quite pretty and nicely demure. They each had matching satin ribbons and strings of tiny pearls woven into their hair, courtesy of Isabella's maid and they did make an interesting picture, the one fair and innocent-looking, the other dark and sultry and, in all honesty, a little obvious. On arrival, Isabella let her shawl slip to her elbows and Cordelia now saw for herself the daring frontage. She also observed how short the sleeves were, leaving an expanse of bare upper arm even above her long gloves, as well as, in her view, the fairly tasteless expanse of chest. Cordelia wore her trusty button-up-to-the-neck silk pelisse with the matching rose in her hair, which was wound atop her head as usual.

The players had taken their places and were tuning up their instruments. Before the concert began, Cordelia decided on a little rearrangement. She stood.

"Here, Isabella, why don't you change places with me and sit next to Felicity? Then you don't have to keep leaning across me."

Isabella duly obliged. It was not really Cordelia's intent to aid their conspiratorial communication, but rather to take Isabella's seat for herself and dispel any hope on the part of the gentleman beside her of engaging her attention. She'd observed his interest right from the moment he'd sat down beside her.

The concert began and the two girls spent the entire time whispering together and Cordelia suspected it was all about various gentlemen they'd spotted in the audience. Afterwards, there was a general movement to walk about for a while until the start of the fireworks.

"Let's go this way," Isabella said, linking Felicity's arm in hers and steering them up the tiered seating to make their way along one side of the rectangular path that edged the gardens. "It will take us up to a good viewpoint for the fireworks by the looks of the number of others going this way."

It also, thought Cordelia, as she followed behind, gave a good view of the crowds below, and whichever gentleman the girl was keen to track this evening. Somehow, the few young men who had dared to call at St James's Square on the morning after a ball were not the ones Isabella wished to see. Cordelia was a little relieved that the callers were invariably for Isabella rather than Felicity, although the latter was naturally somewhat disappointed, especially since that young man with whom she'd been so enamoured had altered his allegiance, despite her substantial inheritance.

The light was fading fast and masses of little coloured lamps were now being lit. That made the scene very picturesque, but the lights were not particularly bright, which no doubt aided the various clandestine meetings that were said to happen in the nooks and crannies of the gardens.

They'd only gone a short distance, when Cordelia, scanning the crowd ahead, was horrified to see those two awful men, Lord Farnham and Viscount Trumble, coming their way, clearly intent on renewing their acquaintance with the two young ladies, whom they'd previously greeted briefly outside St George's church. Cordelia had no idea which was which, but she saw the dark-haired taller one take a quick swig from a silver flask before handing it back to his friend. From their slightly unsteady gait and flushed faces, they must already be in their cups.

Suddenly, Cordelia saw another man, tall and elegant, blond curls showing beneath his top hat and carrying a silver-topped walking cane. She vaguely thought she'd seen him before, but couldn't place him. He'd overtaken the two somewhat slow-moving gentlemen and then, somehow, the taller one, who was closest to him, was on the ground.

"I say, watch your step, old man," the victim said, evidently seeing the cane but not registering the age of its owner, who could surely be no more than five-and-thirty.

"I do beg your pardon, old chap," the man said in an equally refined accent, which however sounded a little contrived. "Allow me to assist you."

"You've done enough of that already," he snapped. "Help me up, Jack," he said to his friend.

"Any bones broken?" the owner of the cane asked. "I'm a surgeon, so if I can offer any treatment. I'm quite handy at amputations." He patted his coat. "Got my saw somewhere hereabouts. We recommend a good tot of rum for the pain, but I think you might already be tanked up sufficiently."

The two girls, with Cordelia immediately behind them, heard the entire exchange, as did a number of other bystanders and there was considerable laughter. The surgeon, if that was who he really was, had diffused the situation with humour and managed to avoid a foolish drunken challenge to a duel, even though Cordelia was convinced he had deliberately positioned his cane between the man's legs to cause him to fall. The two drunken idiots sloped off, the one who'd been tripped complaining of his knee while the other moaned about his empty flask. Then from behind the surgeon, another figure appeared.

"There you are Doc," he called out.

Cordelia recognised the voice before she saw him. It was Captain Stanhope and the tall man was one of his friends. They were within yards of each other.

"Cordelia," he said, with a slight bow of the head. He did not sound surprised to find her here, while to her it was totally unexpected.

"Captain Stanhope," she replied, bobbing a slight curtsy and quite staring at him. She couldn't drag her eyes away. She'd forgotten how handsome he was.

"Ah, the lady from Bond Street, I take it," his tall friend said. "Introductions, Hal, if you please."

It was pretty obvious to |Cordelia that it was Isabella to whom he wished an introduction. She guessed it had been no coincidence that the man had dealt with the unwelcome attentions of those other two. He had surely been intent on approaching their party himself and had deliberately dispatched the rival pair. This must be the man Isabella had been making eyes at across the amphitheatre and he was a friend of Captain Stanhope, who now responded to the request.

"Yes, of course. Ladies, may I present Christopher Garvey, surgeon and chivalrous rescuer of young ladies from drunken louts. We served on board ship together." He then indicated Cordelia with the sweep of one hand. "Doc, this is Lady Cordelia Penshurst, who it seems requires not one but two chaperones."

Everyone laughed and Cordelia then completed the introductions.

"Gentlemen, may I present Lady Felicity Fanshawe and her friend Lady Isabella Daneford. Girls, this is Captain Henry Stanhope."

The girls both curtsied and Cordelia was not surprised to note the way Isabella bobbed somewhat lower and a few seconds longer than necessary, deliberately leaning slightly forward before rising. If they didn't know it already, she was making no mistake to inform them how well-endowed she was.

"Come, ladies," the man called Doc said, "I've organised some refreshments in one of the little alcoves up yonder, from where we should have an excellent view of the fireworks." He proffered an elbow each to the girls. "Shall we?"

The two girls did not need further invitation and slid an arm apiece in his and set off. That left Cordelia alongside Captain Stanhope and they fell into step behind the trio. He didn't take her arm, however, and Cordelia wasn't sure if she was disappointed or relieved. Conversation might help the situation.

"I'm surprised to find you in Town, captain," she began. "I thought you were in Wiltshire for the summer."

"And so I am," he said. "Urgent business brought me to Town for a very brief visit. I only arrived this morning and am returning tomorrow." He lowered his voice. "I was delighted to receive your letter. I had meant to reply but calculated it would not reach you before you also left Town."

"Yes. We are to set out very early on the day after tomorrow," she told him.

"Those two ne'er-do-wells that Doc just dealt with," he said. "Did you realise who they were?"

She had been concentrating on the path, but glanced sideways at his face to find him looking at her. She could quite lose herself in those blue eyes. "My accosters in St James's Street, yes, although I don't know which is which."

"The taller, who fell, is Stephen Trumble. His friend is Jack Farnham."

"So do I take it that your friend Mr Garvey knows of the…er…incident?"

He nodded. "Most of the *haut ton* knows. It was rather public. I trust that doesn't upset you too much."

"Why should it? I have no reputation to lose." She tried to force a light tone into her voice, as if it did not matter at all. "They'll have fun with tonight's occurrence, I imagine. Trumble takes a tumble at the feet of the footman's daughter, or some such."

Somehow, she realised, he knew her half-hearted attempt at a joke was not genuine, for he did not even smile. He took her nearest arm and guided her to one side of the path, coming to a halt and allowing the crowds to amble past them. He let go and then turned to face her, so she was forced to meet his gaze. He did look serious.

"Cordelia, if I *had* replied to your letter, what I intended to say was to applaud you for the way you've gone about taking control of your own life. None of us can help the situation we're placed in, but what we can do is make the best of the life we've got. There will always be those who scoff, who gossip and make fun of others' woes. Let them get their entertainment that way if they please. One wonders how they might view things were your lot theirs. I'm sure I'm not alone in holding you in a good deal of respect for how you've handled things."

He'd held her gaze for the entire time he'd spoken and she could both see and hear his sincerity.

"Thank you," she said at last.

He turned for the path. "Come, let us find the others, before Doc does something he shouldn't." He slipped her arm in his.

She laughed. She probably shouldn't, but she couldn't help it. "You mean you've allowed my two wards to wander off at the mercy of a lothario?"

"At least they're in safe hands, should either require medical attention."

He kept her arm linked in his and it felt lovely to walk beside him and to have his touch. She knew it was hopeless, but she couldn't help it. She'd fallen in love with him. It was impossible that her feelings would be returned, but at least she could count on his friendship. That was precious and she must do nothing to allow him to see her deeper feelings and so drive him away.

They found the other three already partaking of the refreshments and Cordelia at once frowned at the sight of both girls tipping glasses to their mouths. Mr Garvey noticed and disabused her at once.

"Worry not, my lady. It's lemonade. Would you care for some?"

He passed her a glass and poured one for the captain, then raised his own.

"Your health," he said.

They all joined in the toast and then arranged themselves on the curved bench seat, ready to watch the firework display. It was a squash to all fit and the two gentlemen perched at either end, only half on the seat. Cordelia was next to the captain and their thighs were touching. She found her body reacting in all kinds of pleasurable ways. She was reminded of the girls' conversation, overheard in the garden of Fanshawe House, and felt a flush rise up her neck.

At the other end of the bench, she was not surprised that Isabella had made sure she was next to Mr Garvey. To give her credit, she was good fun to have in a party, not at all shy when it came to conversing and quite amusing.

"You know, gentlemen," she said, "you're extremely fortunate to have our company this evening."

"Why so?" her faithful attendant dutifully asked.

"Tell them, Flic," she instructed her friend. That was another thing. She did try to draw her less outgoing friend into proceedings.

"Well, let me see," Felicity began. "There was in fact a choice, although it was no choice at all really. It was the Marchioness of Salisbury's conversazione on the one hand, or the Marchioness of Lansbury's assembly on the other."

"They will both be the same, in effect," Isabella added. "Let's show them Flic." She got to her feet and pulled up her friend. "It looks something like this…"

The two of them put their arms to their sides as though pinioned there, stood stick upright and pressed against each other and their audience duly laughed.

"It reminds me of a gathering at Lord Hertford's place I mistakenly attended," Mr Garvey said "A bit of a crowd."

"Yes, they always are," Isabella said as she and Felicity squeezed back down on the bench. "Like here," she added, fluttering her eyelashes, "except at least here we've somewhere to sit."

"We've learnt to avoid anything containing the words assembly, conversazione or rout," Felicity said. "There's no dancing and hardly any food and you can't hear yourself think."

"Private parties are much more fun," Isabella said. "My parents will be holding a coming out ball in my honour next week when we're back on the estate in Wiltshire. It's a shame you won't be there.

"Wiltshire, you say," Mr Garvey repeated. "Oh, but we shall."

10: On the road

Wednesday 1st July 1812, Bath Road

At Doc's revealing that he and Henry were also bound for Wiltshire, the reaction of the young woman in scarlet was somewhat lost amidst a volley of crackles as the first fireworks lit the evening sky. Henry saw her clap her hands and thought she might have cried out *wonderful*, but whether that was at the prospect of their all travelling to the same county or at seeing fountains of colourful sparks up aloft, he couldn't tell.

The exclamations of the audience and the constant explosions, which reminded Henry too much of guns in battle to enjoy the spectacle, made further conversation impossible. At one particularly loud crack, Henry felt himself start and it was clear Cordelia, so close beside him, had noticed. She glanced up at him with concern and he shrugged and gave a half-hearted smile. She said nothing, but he sensed she understood why this event might not be comfortable for men of military background.

He would have liked to engage her in more conversation, in particular to mention his visit to Lady Dunwoody earlier in the afternoon, but there was no opportunity. Once the display ended, Cordelia, who could evidently be quite firm in her supervisory duties, laid down the law.

"Thank you so much for the refreshments, Mr Garvey," she said. "We shall be meeting our coachman now, shan't we girls? We mustn't be too late tonight. Busy day tomorrow."

Henry could see the crestfallen expressions on both girls' faces. However, they did not demur, but simply echoed Cordelia's thanks. Isabella, however, did get in a question.

"Tell me, Mr Garvey, where should I address the invitation to my ball?"

Henry decided to answer for him, although he was pretty sure his friend was already on the invitation list. His mother would have seen to that.

"He's staying with me, at Stanhope Hall, my lady. I believe my mother and yours are well acquainted. The distance is not far."

The girl was quick, that was for sure, and definitely a practised manipulator.

"In that case," she said, "it would be no trouble at all if you would care to join our carriage party on Wednesday and we can deliver you both right to your door."

Doc gave Henry a questioning look, but left Henry to respond.

"We had been going by the post tomorrow. Are you sure your carriage is large enough?"

"It seats six comfortably," Isabella assured them. "You could send an express at once to let them know you'll be a day late."

Interesting, thought Henry, as he caught his friend's raised brows. Whoever took this voluptuous young woman to bride might have an enjoyable time in bed, but the rest of his life would possibly be organised for him!

It was then that Cordelia intervened, apparently to give them a way out if they wanted it.

"I'm sure that's a kind suggestion, Isabella, but had you not better consult your coachman first? With both your and Felicity's trunks, an additional two passengers might make the load too heavy."

"Nonsense," she replied at once. "He'll do as he's told."

Cordelia had one more try as she glanced from him to Doc. "We are intending to depart quite early in order to get the journey done in the day. I believe we were aiming at half past five in the morning."

Doc answered for both of them. "We're accustomed to shipboard hours. That will be no problem, my lady. I believe your home is in St James's Square, Lady Felicity?" he added.

She nodded. "That's right."

"That is but five minutes from our hotel," he told her, before meeting Cordelia's eye. "And we have virtually no luggage at all."

"That's settled, then," Isabella said, clapping her hands in celebration.

"Let us walk you to your carriage," Henry suggested.

Isabella at once claimed her place beside Doc and Felicity again went on his other side, leaving him to escort Cordelia. It gave him the opportunity to mention his visit to Lady Dunwoody and how pleased his brother had been with the portrait. There was little time for any further exchanges, for the ladies were leaving earlier than most and their carriage was already waiting in the appointed spot without the usual congestion of other vehicles.

They all paused beside the coach to say goodnight and the outspoken Isabella took the opportunity to further demonstrate her snobbery and lack of tact.

"So sorry, gentlemen. We would offer you a lift, but Baronet Fanshawe's carriage is rather small compared to ours. We shall very much look forward to seeing you on Wednesday." She curtsied and allowed Doc to hand her up. He then turned to do the same for Felicity, who, before she stepped up, also had something to say.

"Thank you for your company, Mr Garvey, and for the refreshments. About Wednesday…would you mind coming directly into the mews rather than use the front door, as most of the staff won't be up at that time."

"Of course," Doc said, as he handed her in. Because he was positioned for it, it was natural that he also helped Cordelia up the step. She smiled her thanks and nodded briefly at each of them before Doc closed the door.

They stood by the roadside to watch the carriage roll away.

"Back to the hotel for a snifter?" Doc suggested. "Let's hail a cab, seeing as the snooty Lady Isabella couldn't furnish us with her six-seater carriage this evening."

Henry gave him a light slap on the back. "Isn't she just! But I thought you were interested."

"I'm thirty-five, Hal. Can you see me with a girl like that? She'd have me in my grave by forty! She makes her…appetites rather too obvious for my taste. If I'm going to develop my medical career, especially if I eventually develop my own practice, I need a woman sensible enough to help me in that regard. I certainly don't want a vain, self-seeking and self-absorbed girl, so caught up with her own concerns, she has no awareness of anyone else, nor any tact."

"To hear you speak thus is a revelation, Doc. I thought you had your eye on her all evening."

"The packaging is very alluring," he responded. "But the contents are shallow and disappointing. No, the friend has a good deal more to recommend her."

"But she's also quite young." Henry refrained from mentioning that both were candidates for marriage to him, according to his mother.

"True. At twenty-eight, they'd suit you better, I think. I probably need someone of more mature years."

"Like Lady Cordelia?" Henry suggested.

"She's interesting indeed and nothing like the impression I got of her in that first encounter in Bond Street. I imagine she has been somewhat humbled in having her origins revealed to her, as well as to society in general."

Henry began to be rather sorry he'd confided her story to his friends as he had—not that it wasn't already public knowledge and had been for years. "I don't think she has any expectations of a good marriage, or even a marriage at all."

"That's a shame," Doc said, as he hailed a cab. "She's probably got much to offer in that regard. In fact, I might have thought to make a move myself, were her affections not focused elsewhere."

The cab pulled up beside them and they gave the driver directions and climbed in. "What did you mean by that?" Henry asked, thinking Doc must be privy to some society gossip that had passed him by.

"Sometimes, Hal, I think you are either unobservant or unintelligent, or both. Have you not noticed the way she looks at you?"

Henry shrugged. "As a friend. After all, I did help her out of an awkward situation—more than one in fact." He thought of the purchase of the portrait as well as the incident in St James's Street.

"I suspect it's a lot more than that. The woman's in love with you. It's clear for all to see."

The shock of his friend's conclusion robbed Henry of speech, but his mind was racing and he was thankful the carriage was dark, so Doc couldn't see his confusion. He'd noticed some embarrassment on Cordelia's part when they encountered one another this evening. She'd not been expecting to see him, while he *had* been prepared. He sensed she'd been self-conscious when he took her arm. But all that did not amount to being in love! What was Doc seeing that he wasn't? In the end he found a fairly tame answer.

"Well, she's already taken. If the so-called Marquess of Dartington arrives with his self-made fortune, she'll be walking up the aisle within three weeks."

"That, my friend, is highly unlikely. By all accounts the man perished in some jungle years ago. No, I guess your main obstacle is not a prior betrothal, but the attitude of your somewhat aristocratic family, especially now you're in line for the title."

"I'm too busy learning how to run the estate to think of marriage, Doc. You're welcome to whichever of the three you choose." Even as he said the words, Henry knew it wasn't quite true. He cared a lot what happened to Cordelia Penshurst, but he knew there were insurmountable obstacles to taking her to wife. Now he had the journey to Wiltshire to cope with, sharing the carriage with Cordelia. Seeing her again, he would inevitably dwell on Doc's comments, which in turn would likely cause him to examine Cordelia's behaviour towards him and he was in great danger of reading more into it than was there. He began to consider making some excuse and taking the fast post, as originally planned. But, of course, he didn't.

Dawn on Wednesday found him and Doc walking the short distance to join the ladies' party. To give their travel companions credit, even the vanity-stricken Isabella was ready on time. It was indeed a grand coach, and the coachman had the assistance of a lad who came with the hired team of six horses to act as postillion when needed, and there was also an armed guard. However, from their conversation in the bar last evening, not even all Lord Daneford's ostentatious wealth could persuade Doc to court his daughter. He also avoided sitting beside her, by at once taking charge of the seating arrangements.

"Now then, the three ladies on the facing bench, I think. Hal and I will take the backward facing." He duly handed the two girls in first, but he'd forgotten about Isabella's maid.

"She must sit here in the middle beside me," Isabella insisted. She patted the seat between her and Felicity. "I may need help with this hat. The feather's touching the roof. I don't want it to break."

Doc then turned to Cordelia. "Do you have a preference, my lady—the middle or a window seat?"

Henry was not at all surprised when she at once chose the middle. Doc climbed in first and helped her up. This placed Doc opposite Isabella, while Henry was facing Felicity, with Cordelia opposite the maid, who looked decidedly pleased with herself at having a mistress who did not banish her to an outside seat.

There was little conversation during the first stage of the journey, which would take them to their first change of horses and a good breakfast at Slough. They all rested back their heads and dozed most of the way. That was not so easy for those seated in the middle, who had no padded corner squabs on which to rest their heads. At one point, he was disturbed, as they all must have been, when Isabella woke to find her maid's head resting on her shoulder. "For goodness sake, sit up straight," she told her. "You're crushing my gown." He suspected Cordelia did not really sleep at all. She appeared to be maintaining her position sitting bolt upright in the middle, possibly self-conscious about doing the same as the maid, or in a permanent state of tension about riding in a fairly fast carriage.

It was not until they disembarked at the coaching inn that Henry really took in what the females of the party were wearing. For his part he still wore the dark blue jacket and buff pantaloons with the brown and blue embroidered waistcoat and his brown hessians. The linen ruffles to neck and cuffs gave a smart finishing touch. It was what he'd donned for his formal interview at Somerset House. Good lord! Was that only two days ago, the point at which his life had taken an about-turn?

Unsurprisingly, Lady Isabella had on a carriage costume in the height of fashion—that is, according to her that was the case! She kept her maid busy.

"I need my Spencer, girl," she fussed, as she stepped down. "I can't wear the hat without it—it makes the hat look too dark." She had on a muslin dress dotted with dark red flowers and the plain jacket and hat were of a toning burgundy, as were her half boots. It certainly was a fashionable-looking outfit compared to the fairly simple muslin dresses worn by the other two, which however looked far more sensible wear for travel. Inevitably, Isabella fussed about having to climb down onto the dusty ground outside the yard. Another carriage was ahead of them being re-harnessed with a fresh team of horses and they had to wait their turn.

The driver was apologetic and quite annoyed, for he'd booked them in.

"Not to worry," Henry said. "More time for breakfast."

On entering the place, Doc requested the private room, but was informed it was already taken and would they mind using the public dining room. They would have it to themselves at present, he assured them. Hot dishes were soon laid before them, of ham, eggs and potatoes and a pot of tea and they helped themselves. Henry could not help but notice how little Cordelia spooned onto her plate and he wanted to encourage her to have more. Knowing how difficult she found coach travel, it would be better to have a full stomach than an empty one, in his opinion, but he said nothing, for there was no opportunity to speak with her alone.

The Lady Isabella had no inhibitions at table, as in life in general. She began by arranging the seating around the oval table so that she was positioned between him and Doc. Once the food arrived, she pronounced on the amount of fat on the meat, the freshness of the eggs, the staleness of the bread and the temperature of the tea and how much more preferable it was to dine at home on provisions from one's own cook and kitchens. The young man who'd been serving them heard it all.

To Henry's surprise, it was Cordelia who commented on the girl's tactless manner and in a way he'd never have expected. She used sarcasm, although it was probably quite lost on the self-absorbed young woman. Laying down her fork, having cleared the little she'd put on her plate, Cordelia looked across at Isabella, who'd consumed considerably more.

"I see Felicity has finished her meal, Isabella" she said. "If you have now also had sufficient—despite your estimation of the quality of the food—perhaps you would like to find your maid and both accompany me to the yard to make use of the facilities before we get on our way." She did not wait for a response but stood and made for the door. They had little choice but to follow.

Henry looked at Doc, who was shaking his head. "It gets worse," he muttered and got to his feet. "Let's check out the carriage."

They found it ready to depart.

"Apologies for the delay, gentlemen," the stableman said. "Had some big wig from the navy to see to first. On 'is way to Bath, so if that's your route, you'll probably meet him again, though with six horses you might well overtake him."

"I'll make sure we do," the Daneford coachman replied. "I know just the stretch, a few miles before Reading, well-graded road and quite wide."

True to his word the man's plan was executed. They'd been behind the other carriage for a few miles, keeping a good distance in order to avoid the dust. Then Henry felt them accelerate and they soon drew level with the other coach. A glance at Cordelia, beside him, confirmed what he'd anticipated. Her hands were gripping the edges of the cushion and she was pressing her back against the padding, her eyes tight shut, although none of them could shut out the thundering of the horses' hooves as they got up speed. He wanted to place a hand over hers to reassure her, but that would draw everyone's attention to her state of panic. He could see the maid was already watching her.

Inevitably, Isabella notice nothing, being too busy watching the other carriage. She became quite animated as they drew level with it.

"Oh, this is just like those four-in-hand races they hold along the Row!" she exclaimed. "Isn't it exciting?"

Being on the left of their coach, Henry had a clear view of the Royal Navy coat of arms on the side of the coach, as theirs edged past it. He wondered for a moment whether he might know the dignitary on board, but as the other vehicle's front-facing seat came into view, he saw a woman seated there. She, in turn, was examining their carriage and their eyes met. Good lord, he thought, I might have guessed. Mrs Frances Williams was on board! He knew from his own experience just how adept she was at persuading a gentleman to invite her for a ride in his carriage and wondered just which navy man had been beguiled into the role this time. She'd clearly recognised Henry and immediately broke the eye contact and gave no acknowledgement, but her companion must have noticed something.

He was seated opposite her and now came into Henry's view. Henry saw only his profile, heavy jowls with long side-whiskers. He'd evidently asked her a question, for he swivelled his head and looked directly at Henry and touched a hand to his gold-braided admiral's cocked hat. Henry nodded in return, before focusing back inside their own carriage. He didn't know the man but he was clearly quite senior and at least old enough to be the lady's father. Neither of them would be aware he was actually no longer in the service, unless the admiral was one of those based at naval headquarters. At his age, he might well be. A glance across at Doc told him his friend was checking something in his pocket book and had not noticed the Williams woman.

They soon left the slower coach behind them and neared Reading, where they were booked in for lunch at The George Inn. Their driver encouraged them to eat as quickly as possible, since he wanted to get on. Thus, despite the inevitable protestations from Lady Isabella, they were on the road again in under a half hour and turned out from the inn onto the road just as the Royal Navy carriage was approaching.

There were no further encounters or holdups and they reached Stanhope Hall a little after four. Henry felt he had no choice but to invite the ladies in for refreshments, so they all disembarked at the front portico and Henry directed the coachman to the stable block to refresh the horses as well as himself and his men. The express he'd sent to his mother had informed her that he would come a day later than planned, but he'd not explained the reason. He had no doubt what her reaction would be once she realised he had travelled with her two favourite candidates for her next daughter-in-law!

11: Stanhope Hall

Wednesday evening, 1st July 1812, Wiltshire

Cordelia could see quite clearly that Felicity and Isabella were delighted at being invited to break the final part of their journey here at Stanhope Hall. As for herself, apart from the relief she ever experienced at disembarking safely from a carriage, her feelings were somewhat less enthusiastic. Every moment she spent in Henry's company served to remind her how hopeless were her feelings for him and now she must be careful not to give herself away by a look or a word in front of his family. In addition was the unpalatable truth that they'd been on the road for almost twelve hours. This had consequences, chief amongst them being that their gowns were creased and hardly as fresh as one would normally expect when visiting a viscount's household—neither, come to that, were their bodies!

Cordelia had worn one of her faithful old muslin gowns in the plain white so fashionable a few years back. It was much washed and a fairly loose weave, as well as a comfortably loose fit. Thus, she had kept reasonably cool during the journey, despite how her closeness to Captain Stanhope had heated her blood. He wore some fairly subtle cologne, a pleasant citrus aroma. How strange it was, being welcomed into his family home like this, when she would, in the normal course of events, never step across its portals.

The house was unexpected, for it was neither as old nor as large as she'd anticipated. It was also quite plain on the outside. She recognised the Georgian architecture with the many-paned sash windows. There were only two main floors, with seven bays across the front. Altogether, it was hardly bigger that Baronet Fanshawe's town house, except here there were numerous outbuildings, which she'd glimpsed as they approached, including, close by, a substantial church with a square tower about the same height as the main house.

A footman rushed out to see to the carriage door and let down the steps on Mr Garvey's side. He immediately stepped out and handed down all the ladies, Cordelia being the last. She was embarrassed, but hardly surprised, to catch the end of Isabella's comment, spoken in her usual thoughtless manner. She was standing, arms akimbo, staring up at the building.

"…quite forgotten how small this place is compared to Daneford Court…and so very plain." The comment also informed Cordelia that the two households were acquainted, but she'd not got the impression that the captain had met Isabella before. After all, she'd had to make the introductions the other night at the Vauxhall Gardens. A little arithmetic soon told her that Isabella would have been an eight-year-old in the school room when the captain first went to sea at the age of eighteen. But he might possibly have known the eldest sister.

The captain stepped out of the carriage behind Cordelia and, she trusted, had not overheard the tactless Isabella's remarks. But then she caught the look exchanged between him and Mr Garvey—raised brows and pursed lips—and knew it was a vain hope.

The double front doors stood open and a black-suited man of middle years, whom she took for the butler, was waiting just inside. The captain went up the steps ahead of the party and entered the hall.

"Welcome home, sir," the man greeted him, inclining his head.

"Thank you, Mr Collins." The captain indicated the rest of the party with the sweep of one hand. "I do not come alone, as you see. Mr Garvey, you had notice of. He and I were fortunate enough to share Lady Isabella's carriage for the journey. She and her companions are making for Daneford Court but first, could you organise some tea and ask Mrs Rackham to conduct the three ladies to a suitable chamber to refresh themselves. And forewarn my mother that she has some additional guests."

"Yes, sir. You'll find her and the Lady Dora in the drawing room."

Mr Garvey crooked his elbows and offered one each to the two young ladies and conducted them up the steps and through the portal. Cordelia followed alongside the maid. As soon as she entered, she could not but be struck by the contrast between the appearance of the exterior and the décor inside the huge hall. It was an oblong of at least, she estimated, fifty feet in length. But it was the finish that was so striking. The high ceiling was densely-covered in ornate plasterwork and there were equally ornate carvings forming elegant silhouettes on the on walls. Even Isabella gasped, and apparently had nothing immediate to say.

At one end, a broad, cantilevered staircase rose to the landing above. Cordelia went closer to examine it. The slim mahogany handrail was supported by the slender curves and swirls of decorative ironwork in black and gold, but it was the wooden treads that struck her most of all. She'd never seen their like. They were made up of small oblong blocks of all shades of brown plus black and white, arranged in a matching pattern on each tread. She bent down to feel the surface and found it quite smooth with no hint of any edges of the many different pieces that made up the pattern. She could only imagine the work that must have gone into its construction. So absorbed was she by the wonderful design of the place that she forgot to be self-conscious. Nor did she notice what the others were doing until the captain's voice drew her attention. He'd come over to join her.

"People visit merely to see the staircase," he told her. "The marquetry's astonishing, isn't it? It's by Lightfoot, the same man who designed the Rococo decorations you'll see everywhere. The white strips on the stairs are inlaid ivory."

Embarrassed, she made a move to rise and found the captain reaching out a hand to help her. "I do beg your pardon," she muttered, so aware of his touch and feeling the blush rising up her cheeks.

He did not respond to that and she thought perhaps he'd not heard her, as he let go of her hand and turned to the rest of the party.

"Excuse us," he said. "Doc and I are going to freshen up. The housekeeper, Mrs Rackham, will conduct your party to a suitable chamber where you can do likewise, then she'll escort you to the drawing room for some tea."

At the other end of the hall, where a staircase must lead down to the various service rooms, a middle-aged woman in a neat grey gown, whom she took for the housekeeper, was instructing a housemaid who'd been summoned from somewhere. Then she indicated for Felicity, Isabella and her maid to follow her to the foot of the staircase. Cordelia fell into step behind them.

The two gentlemen were already striding along the landing and were soon out of sight, which was just as well, given Isabella's tongue. She was examining one of the decorative panels on the wall and stroking it. "So fussy," she commented, as she then moved across to the stair rail and touched the metalwork. "This must be the devil to dust. If I lived here, I'd modernise the place."

Cordelia felt like commenting *fortunate for you you're not a housemaid,* but held her tongue. Upstairs, they were led to a small chamber at the back of the house and found three maids were just coming away from the room, having delivered three jugs of water. It was a most efficiently-run house. She guessed this was used as a guest-room. It was decorated on the theme of lemon-yellow, red and cream, reflected in the wallpaper, the hearth rug and the rather beautiful embroidered satin canopy on the mahogany bed frame. The room was beautifully light, situated on a corner with a doubt aspect of windows.

"But I've nothing to change into," Isabella said, in that whining tone she adopted on complaining of anything inconvenient. Cordelia was beginning to lose patience.

"Isabella, we are remaining for not more than a half hour to drink tea. Your parents are expecting us at Daneford Court. There is no time to unload trunks and find a fresh outfit. Make the best of it. See they've provided wash cloths and a towel for each of us." She picked up the cake of soap by one bowl and put it to her nose. "And this is rose-scented soap. I'm going to strip off my gown and wash the parts I can reach and then put it back on. It should take less than twenty minutes. Come on, now, are you not curious to meet Captain Stanhope's mother?"

That last remark did the trick and they were soon ready, even allowing for a brief tidying of their hair by the maid, whom Isabella treated abominably. She persistently called her *girl,* when she must be close to forty if she was a day. Neither did she do her the courtesy of addressing her by name. It was not Cordelia's place to deal with such unpleasant behaviour, but she'd very much like to have had the authority to do so. Instead, she pointedly thanked the woman as they left the room.

Thank you for your help, Serina," she said. "I expect there'll be refreshments for you downstairs." The woman gave an appreciative smile and turned for the servants' stairs, which descended from close by, while the three duly refreshed ladies made their way along the landing, where they met the housekeeper coming to find them. The two gentlemen awaited them in the hall, both sporting formal dark evening-wear, although neither would have had time to shave, so the captain, in particular, had a dark shadow across his jaw, which was far from unattractive.

On entering the drawing room, Cordelia once more found her eyes drawn upwards. The cavernous ceiling was covered in more ornate plasterwork. She let her eyes run over it before being drawn down to the door surrounds and fireplace, whose equally ornate carving echoed the designs in the hall. The walls were embossed in a medium blue paper and contrasted nicely with the white carvings and ceiling. A grand piano in one corner was quite dwarfed by the dimensions of the room.

"Magnificent!" she exclaimed, staring all around. Suddenly, she realised that the two girls and Mr Garvey had already crossed the room and were being introduced by Captain Stanhope to two ladies, who'd just risen from the sofa at the far end. Stop behaving like a tourist visiting a grand house, she told herself, as she stepped in their direction. Evidently, the older lady had heard Cordelia's gasp of admiration, for she nodded and smiled at Cordelia.

"Yes, isn't it? Rococo by Lightfoot, one of the top designers," she said. "I'm not sure it would have been my taste, but my father-in-law, the second viscount, was very keen. He's the one who had the place built and selected the décor."

"It's very impressive," Cordelia said, realising she'd not yet been introduced so could not use the lady's name.

Captain Stanhope immediately stepped her way, captured her nearest hand and led her closer to the group, before letting go.

"Mother…Dora…allow me to present the Lady Cordelia Penshurst, granddaughter of the late Lord Charles Elderfold. Cordelia, this my mother Viscountess Stanhope and my sister-in-law, the Honourable Dora Stanhope."

They all three curtsied and Cordelia noted how unlike her son the viscountess was, with pale blue eyes and greying hair that still showed hints of the blonde it had once been, in contrast to the darker blue eyes and dark colouring of her youngest son. He and his eldest brother must take after their father. Thinking of likenesses reminded her of the picture. The walls were hung with quite a lot family portraits and she glanced around, seeking it. She soon picked it out and Dora's eyes followed the direction of her gaze.

"Of course!" Dora exclaimed, stepping towards it and standing right beneath her husband's likeness. "Godfrey's portrait! We can't thank you enough, my lady."

Cordelia sensed curiosity coming from the Daneford girl. Felicity was aware of Cordelia's background, but had evidently not shared that knowledge with her friend, nor mentioned the tale of the stolen portrait. As far as Isabella was concerned, Cordelia was some poor relation having to earn her living. In reality, apart from her dubious paternity, Cordelia was the same status as Isabella. Both were descended from an earl. Expecting to be quizzed further by the supercilious girl, Cordelia was quite surprised to find Isabella had apparently been stunned to silence.

"I'm sure my husband will be sorry to have missed you all," the viscountess said, "and Godfrey, too. They're making a tour of the estate to…"

She left the sentence unfinished and Cordelia noticed a searching look from mother to son. What was that about?

It was Isabella who, having apparently recovered from the shock of learning about Cordelia's heritage, now filled the silence.

"We'll all meet again at Daneford Court," she announced, in a jolly tone. "The invitations for my coming-out ball will be sent soon. We visited a wonderful modiste in Town, did we not, Flic? I've got a beautiful new gown for the occasion. I shan't spoil the surprise by telling you any more about it."

"We shall very much look forward to seeing you in it," the viscountess said. Her voice was warm, but Cordelia thought the woman's smile a little forced.

It was helpful at that moment that two maids bearing trays entered the room and the remainder of the visit was largely occupied with the routine of pouring and drinking the tea and eating cake, during which Lady Dora invited Cordelia to take a tour around the room looking at the other portraits.

"Both my parents-in-law sat for Mr Hoppner," she said. "They're at the far end there. He did capture likenesses so well."

Cordelia duly allowed herself to be guided around the room and have various ancestors pointed out to her, before lingering at the far end.

"Of course, they were painted some years ago," Dora said.

Cordelia saw at once how alike the viscount was to his eldest son, including the brown eyes. No wonder the captain had recognised the sitter. She could also see the viscountess in this younger version, with golden hair and fewer lines to her face. As they wandered back to the rest of the party Dora had more to say.

"I'm so pleased to meet you, Cordelia, and it's very fitting that you are now entering into society. Henry gave us to understand that you were quite shabbily treated by your relatives."

Cordelia wondered exactly what the captain had conveyed to his family about her circumstances. She decided to disabuse the lady at once. "I'm hardly entering society, my lady, merely working for a living to shepherd my young charge into the fold, so to speak."

"She's very sweet. Her friend, on the other hand…"

They were now within earshot of the rest of the party, so there was no opportunity for Cordelia to respond, which was probably just as well!

It became clear to Cordelia that Isabella had no intention of taking responsibility for drawing their visit to a close, so she decided to take action. Putting down her cup, she glanced meaningfully at the girls, before addressing the viscountess.

"It's been such a pleasure to break our journey here, my lady," she said, before switching her attention to Isabella. "Now we really must set out for your parents' house, Isabella, do you not agree? They might begin to be concerned that we've not yet arrived and it's been a long day for the driver and his men, not to mention for ourselves."

With that, she stood, so forcing the issue. First Felicity and then, clearly reluctantly, Isabella, edged forward on their seats and pushed themselves up. Their hostess and the rest of the party did the same. Cordelia allowed a second or two for one of the girls to perform the social niceties, but Felicity appeared to be a little overawed by her surroundings, whilst Isabella was busy trying to catch Mr Garvey's eye.

"Thank you again for your hospitality, my lady," Cordelia said. "It has been so nice to make your acquaintance and see something of your lovely home." It must be fairly obvious to their hostess that she was delivering a lecture in social niceties to her two charges. She decided not to allow them to get away with saying nothing, so added, "Has it not, girls?"

It was Felicity who be-stirred herself first. "Yes, of course. Thank you so much."

Suddenly deciding she was not to be outdone, Isabella also spoke, but Cordelia noted she was neither looking at, nor addressing, their hostess. She was focused on Mr Garvey, as she had been for most of the visit.

"We do so much look forward to seeing you at my ball," she began. "Perhaps we might meet you before that, Flic and I shall probably go riding, weather permitting."

Neither gentleman responded and the captain walked across to the bell pull to summon the butler, who appeared at once, evidently waiting outside the door. Henry ordered the man to summon their carriage and have the maid called from below stairs. The ladies all curtsied and Mr Garvey bowed and Henry then escorted the three of them into the huge hall and across to the door. Serina soon joined them, but the carriage took a little longer to drive round from the stables. The two girls stood together looking at the view and Isabella was evidently pointing out the direction in which Daneford Court lay.

That left Cordelia standing a little to one side with Henry. She felt awkward, wanting to say how much she'd enjoyed meeting his mother and Dora, but not wanting such a remark to be misinterpreted. In the end he broke the silence.

"It's nice to know there is one convert to Rococo style amongst our visitors," he said, in a quiet voice. "I gather others were not so impressed."

"Whatever one's personal taste," she said, "one cannot but admire the craftsmanship of such work."

"Indeed so."

The carriage now appeared and drew up by the steps. Henry went to open the door and handed the four of them in.

"We'll look forward to meeting again in due course," he said.

"Oh yes, at my ball," exclaimed Isabella.

So they moved off. No doubt their host would return to the drawing room to join in discussing Isabella's tactless and self-centred approach to life, the inept social skills of the two young ladies and Cordelia's own failure at instilling proper behaviour.

As the carriage pulled away, Cordelia hoped Isabella might be circumspect in her comments, given the presence of her maid, but apparently she had no inhibitions about speaking her truth and shaming the devil.

"Well," she began, "that was interesting, was it not?"

"It's certainly an interesting house and the décor is evidently of great architectural interest," Cordelia remarked, knowing full well that the girl had no wish to talk about the building, but rather the people in it.

"Oh, poo to that. My useless maid here is good for something. Tell us the gossip from below stairs, girl!" Serina was sharing the back-facing seat with Cordelia this time and she turned to meet Cordelia's eye, an expression of wide-eyed panic on her face.

"It's not appropriate to put Serina in such an embarrassing position, Isabella. Servants should not gossip and, if she has been put in the awkward situation of overhearing something, she is sensible enough to keep it to herself. Isn't that right, Serina?"

The woman nodded, but Isabella lent forward, her face far from pretty, being screwed up in a frown. "Just remember who pays your wages, girl. Now tell us what you heard."

With a hopeless look at Cordelia, the woman evidently felt forced to oblige. Cordelia wondered in what other circumstances her mistress had employed the threat of dismissal to get her own way on something.

"All the talk was of the changes to the household, my lady."

"Changes?"

Serina nodded. "Lady Dora and her husband are moving abroad for her health and Captain Stanhope's going to be the one to inherit."

"What!" Isabella exclaimed. "But he's in the navy."

"Not any more, my lady. That's why he went up to London. He's resigned his commission."

12: County society

July 1812, Wiltshire

Having seen off the Daneford Court party, Henry returned to the drawing room to find the other three sitting in silence. No doubt they all had something to say about the visit, but a servant was still present.

"Have you all had sufficient?" his mother asked.

They all assented and she instructed the maid to see to the tea things. By common consent no one spoke until the table had been cleared and the door closed. It was his mother who began. She met Henry's eye, her brows raised and her lips pursed.

"Well, Henry, I have now somewhat amended my hopes for your future."

"Ha…should I be trembling in my boots or relieved?"

"Perhaps that depends on how you came to be riding in the Daneford carriage," Dora said. "Is there some understanding between you and either of the young ladies?"

"Not at all," Henry told her.

Doc chipped in then. "Oh, it was entirely the Lady Isabella's doing, but you should not concern yourself unduly, my lady. It's me she has her eye on."

"Yes, so I observed," his mother said. "Do I take it congratulations are in order?"

"Not yet," Doc said. "I shall duly expect good wishes and felicitations plied upon me when I finally escape her clutches!"

Everyone laughed.

"What about the other one…Felicity?" Dora said. "She seems sweet enough and fairly biddable."

"She also comes with thirty thousand pounds," his mother said.

"Does she indeed?" Doc said. "You didn't mention that, Hal."

"I can't imagine why that circumstance would be of interest, my friend," Henry responded.

"It's a good deal more than her friend's marriage portion," his mother added. "It's said Daneford's estate is barely in profit and of course he has that enormous, ostentatious house to staff and maintain. In Felicity's case, the burden is her father. The impecunious Baronet Fanshawe is addicted to gambling and no doubt hopes a future son-in-law will soon become addicted to maintaining him."

"Lady Cordelia is very pleasant," Dora said. "But I think she's on a hopeless campaign to instil any manners or tact in the Daneford girl."

"Fortunately for her, the Lady Isabella does not fall within her remit," Henry said. "She's only responsible for Lady Felicity."

"That may be," his mother said, "but it can't have been easy trying to prevent Lady Isabella from becoming an extremely bad influence."

"True," Doc said, "but I think Isabella is the type to use her so-called friends as a foil to enhance her own chances of being noticed. She's clearly very much up-to-date with the latest ladies' fashions, while her friend seems to go for simpler and certainly less revealing outfits. You should have seen what the shameless Isabella wore to Vauxhall Gardens on Monday night."

"You were at Vauxhall Gardens!" Dora exclaimed. "Oh, do tell us about it. It's supposed to be far grander than Sydney Gardens in Bath, especially after all the improvements they made this year."

So the conversation diverted from a discussion of the recently departed visitors and Henry was quite glad of it. The more he witnessed Cordelia's maturity and competence in social situations, the greater his awareness of the inadvisability of wooing an eighteen-year-old like Felicity or Isabella. The former was pleasant enough, but had no depth to her, whilst the latter would, he suspected, be an embarrassment to any husband. Travelling in the Daneford carriage, plus the sojourn in his own family's drawing room that had inevitably followed, had been most fortuitous, for it had resulted in his mother making it quite clear that she'd ruled out the girl as a future daughter-in-law!

On the other hand, Henry himself was becoming increasingly aware that the more he got to know Cordelia and observed her in society, the more admiration he felt for the way she conducted herself. She would make an ideal wife for a man with a position to maintain. What a waste for her to spend her life in employment as a companion and chaperone. He was saved further regret by reminding himself that his mother would never consider someone of her birth suitable, particularly as he was now in line to inherit his father's title.

He'd left it to Doc to describe the scenes at Vauxhall Gardens and Dora oo'd and ah'd at the description of Monday night's display. But then she glanced his way, tipping her head in a question. "You seem far away, Hal."

"Not at all," he said, immediately grasping at something to say. "I was only wondering whether you will miss mixing in society. I doubt there'll be much going on for British residents in Madeira."

"Perhaps not," she said. "On the other hand, we shall be very busy with the hotel, which I expect will to some degree have a social aspect. I doubt we'll have much spare time for anything else."

"Have you set a date for departure yet?" Doc asked.

Dora glanced quickly from him back to Henry. "Godfrey was going to discuss it with you, Henry."

Henry thought for a moment she was going to say more, but she either wasn't, or she changed her mind. It left him wondering whether they'd booked their passage already, but she was leaving it for Godfrey to tell him. It turned out he was correct on both counts. The ladies soon excused themselves to change for dinner and Henry poured himself and Doc a pre-dinner whisky. Left to themselves, Doc brought the topic of conversation back to the young ladies who'd just departed.

"You know, Hal," Doc began, "I'm now seriously contemplating the Fanshawe girl."

Henry sipped his drink and narrowed his eyes. "For the money?"

"Cynic! I cannot deny it's a huge attraction, but it's not only that. Unlike her friend I think I can trust she's…intact. Plus she's innocent enough to be moulded and I like her well enough. And she's not unintelligent. I think she has the ability to contribute to my medical practice, if she is so inclined…administration and so forth. However, I'm not sure I'm cut out for love and endless faithfulness."

Henry had no time to reply, for at that moment the door opened and Mr Collins appeared and held open the door for his father and brother, who were both also changed and ready for dinner.

"Ah, here you are," his father said. "This must be Doc, whom I've heard so much about."

He and Doc got to their feet and Henry introduced his friend to both men properly.

"I see you're ahead of us," his father said, and nodded at Collins, who poured two more drinks and proffered the tray to Henry's father and brother. "Thank you, Mr Collins, that's all for now," he added, dismissing the man. "Your health," he said, and they all raised their glasses.

Henry decided to ask his question before the ladies joined them.

"Godfrey, am I right in suspecting that…er…there has been some progress in your and Dora's plans? And, please feel free to talk in front of Doc. He's aware of the situation."

With a quick glance their father's way, Godfrey drew a breath to reply. "Well, yes. In fact today's tour of the estate was by way of making my farewells. We sail on Friday. A passage on a frigate came up and we'll be setting out for Portsmouth first thing that morning."

"That's in two days! So soon!" Henry exclaimed. He'd thought he had more time to adjust to this new role of his.

"We'd not planned it thus," Godfrey said. "It's simply that the opportunity materialised. I thought you and I might take a farewell ride tomorrow."

Henry glanced at Doc.

"Worry not about me, my friend," Doc said, clearly getting the message that Godfrey wanted the ride to be with Henry alone. "If I can also be found a horse I shall pay my respects at Daneford Court. It will be interesting to see the place after hearing so much about it."

"Of course," Henry's father said. "I shall furnish you with directions, as well as a mount. We see quite a bit of Lord and Lady Daneford."

"And please don't expect me back in time for dinner," Doc added. "I fully intend to get myself invited to dine there!"

Henry gave Doc a knowing look whilst at the same time having the thought that both he and Doc had also seen a considerable amount of his lordship's youngest daughter!

The following day, all the men took an early breakfast before setting out on their day's occupations. For their part, Henry and Godfrey took their mounts slowly, so they could talk. Much of their discourse was a sharing of memories of younger years, rather than a discussion on the issues around the estate, although they were briefly mentioned.

"Father keeps very well, of course," Godfrey said. "It will be some years before the mantle passes to you, unless—perish the thought—that changes. There will be plenty of time to learn the ropes."

"I'm glad to hear it," Henry said. "Before all this arose, I had been giving some thought to life after the navy and it very much sounds as though I shall still have time to pursue my inclinations."

"Which are?"

"I had thoughts of standing for parliament."

"Really?" said Godfrey, clearly surprised. "You'll gain a seat in the Lords once you inherit."

"I know, but that will be years away. I'd rather get myself elected to the Commons."

"Are any of the Wiltshire boroughs likely to have a vacancy?"

"Oh, I wasn't thinking of standing here. No, I rather thought of Surrey. This is not something I've mentioned, but I've done well out of the navy and I've invested in a small property there. It's within easy reach of Town and a reasonably easy day's travel here, so I would split my time between the two places, depending on when parliament was sitting."

"I wish you well with that. I'm not sure how Father will feel about it."

"Ah…I know. I've not let it be known, even to Doc. I'd rather we kept it between ourselves for now, if you don't mind, both the property and my intentions. Time enough to make Father aware when I actually put myself forward as a candidate, which in turn depends upon when a vacancy occurs."

"Of course, understood. And there is a third place to visit. You must come and see us in Madeira once we're settled."

"I fully intend to!"

As he'd predicted, Doc did not arrive back until sundown, well after the residents of Stanhope Hall had dined. Henry's parents were by then occupied with last-minute tasks to do with Godfrey and Dora's departure in the morning, so Henry invited his friend to share a whisky. They established themselves in the comfort of the drawing room and Henry gave Doc a quizzical look.

"Well?"

Doc smiled. "I've had a most interesting day." Before saying more, he reached inside his coat pocket. "Before I forget, I've been charged with delivering our official invitation to lady Isabella's coming out ball."

He placed it on the table between them and Henry reached across to pick it up and read it.

"The eleventh. That's only a week from Saturday."

"Indeed," said Doc. "I was given a tour of the principal rooms that will be used on the occasion. It's certainly a monstrous large place."

"And has the Lady Isabella booked you for the opening dances?" Henry asked, with a smile.

"Ah, actually, she has not and I've taken the opportunity of asking Lady Felicity to do me that honour."

"Which she accepted, no doubt. Was that in front of her friend? She'd have been somewhat put out, I imagine."

Doc shook his head. "No, actually. I managed to get Felicity alone in a fairly secluded part of the garden."

"You did! How did that go?"

"That's between me and her, but suffice it to say that her friend's former interest in yours truly has thankfully abated, because she's set her sights elsewhere."

Henry gave a short laugh. "Ha! You must be highly relieved. Who's the lucky man?"

"I doubt you'll much like it when you hear. She seems to have ideas of becoming the next Viscountess Stanhope!"

Even as his friend spoke, Henry suspected what he was going to hear. Damnation! At least his mother would be on his side. Of his father's attitude he was less certain, for he was a particular friend of Lord Daneford's. Henry pursed his lips and shook his head.

"Well, I suppose I shall have to attend this wretched ball, but I'm damned if I'm getting caught in any secluded garden with the Lady Isabella."

"Very wise," Doc said. "Now, before that grand event, there is an outing planned for the Wednesday. Lady Daneford wishes to go to Bath for some accoutrements to her daughter's ball outfit and her own. Flic will obviously accompany them."

Henry raised his brows. "Flic, is it now?" he said.

"Why not? Thus, of course, Lady Cordelia must go too. That leave two places in that substantial carriage. I am to take one, as their escort for the day and they hope you will be agreeable to taking the other. That is, Isabella in particular said something about valuing your advice, since you dress with such style yourself!"

"Well I shall not be coming. I have a lot of estate matters to run through with my father. I would be most grateful if you would convey my excuses on the day, but before that say nothing about the planned excursion within my parents' hearing."

"Your mother would not expect you to go, surely. She can't bear the girl."

"But my father might. I do not wish him to be given the option."

"Understood. Mum's the word."

Henry put down his empty glass and rose to his feet. "Now, Doc, if you don't mind, I'm going up now. I want to be able to say my farewells to Godfrey and Dora and they depart extremely early. Do linger as long as you like, help yourself to another drink."

"I will if you don't mind. A few things on my mind I want to ponder. I doubt I'll be up to see off the travellers. Please wish them well from me."

"Will do. Goodnight."

It was with very mixed feelings that Henry witnessed Godfrey and Dora's departure at sunrise the following morning and, if that was true for him, how much more so must it be for his parents and for Godfrey himself. But, as was their wont, neither of them gave much hint as to how they were feeling, except his mother's eyes were a little bright. For his part, Henry felt conflicting emotions. He was sad for their failure to produce children and for the damage to Dora's health from all the attempts. He was a little anxious about the knowledge and skills he would need to develop to follow in his father's footsteps and self-conscious about the comparisons likely to be made between him and his very able eldest brother. At the same time he was quite excited at the prospect of developing a political career in due course. Before any of that happened there was one thing he needed to do. He must find a suitable wife as soon as possible, not least to avoid unwelcome advances by young ladies like Isabella.

He was to hear something of the young lady when Doc reported back on the outing to Bath on his return quite late on Wednesday evening. He joined Henry for a drink before retiring.

"How was the trip?" Henry asked him.

"I'd say it accomplished all that was intended, except Lady Isabella referred on more than one occasion how she was missing *your* company, Hal."

"I hope that did not spoil the outing for anyone else."

Doc smiled. "Which—your absence or her complaining? I don't think so, for there were compensations."

"Do tell," Henry said, curious.

"You know how busy Bath can be at this time of year. As you can imagine, the *haut ton* was much in evidence, particularly when we spent an hour or so in the Assembly Rooms. There I encountered an elderly admiral I knew—not seen him for years—fairly decrepit and now has a part-time administrative role at Somerset House. He was accompanied by a much younger lady and introduced me. Can you guess?"

"Lieutenant Samuel Williams' widow. How fortunate I did not accompany you to Bath!"

"Quite. I did not gather the basis on which they were together, but I'd say the gentleman looked a little uncomfortable. We also encountered two other gentlemen who are known to us both—known only in the sense that I'm aware of their names. They are not friends. Can you not guess?"

"Surely not Farnham and Trumble?"

"The very same. They'd clearly at some point discovered my name and thus felt at liberty to make the approach. Their purpose, naturally, was to re-acquaint themselves with the young ladies. Trumble planted himself right in front of me. *I see you've neglected to bring your cane today, Doctor Garvey,* he says. Now Lady Daneford had already mentioned her concern at a possible shortage of gentlemen at her daughter's ball."

"How interesting," Henry said. "An indication perhaps that the males of Wiltshire wish to avoid falling into her clutches."

"Quite possibly," Doc said. "Anyway, Lady Daneford at once asks me to make introductions and is delighted to learn that Isabella and Flic are already acquainted with the gentlemen, albeit without having learnt their names. Trust Isabella to bend the truth. *Oh, but we've often seen each other at St George's Church, at morning worship*, she announces. Given that her stay in the capital apparently encompassed just one such Sunday it was a considerable exaggeration and I only had to catch Cordelia's raised eye-brows to become aware of the fact. After hearing that, Lady Daneford wastes no time in inviting them to the ball. Having now gleaned the fact that one is a viscount and the other an earl, Isabella quickly reinforces her mother's invitation. *Oh, do say you'll come*, she says, using that sultry tone she puts on when trying to be charming. Meanwhile, as you might expect, Lady Cordelia is looking most uncomfortable and has stepped slightly behind Lady Daneford to try and evade notice and no one appears to realise that I left her out of the introductions."

"So there's no avoiding these two ne'er-do-wells on Saturday," Henry said, fully intending to set himself up as Cordelia's protector if necessary. Thus far, he suspected, they'd been too busy ogling the two young ladies to pay any attention to their chaperone and had not recognised her as the maid they'd accosted.

13: Daneford Court ball

Saturday 11th July 1812, Wiltshire

To say that Cordelia was not looking forward to this ball was an understatement. She was quite dreading it, to the extent her stomach ached and she had quite lost her appetite. The principal reason for this was not her usual sense of inadequacy at society events, nor the fact that she had nothing suitable to wear, but the dreadful truth that Lord Farnham and Viscount Trumble would be attending.

Thus far they had not recognised Cordelia as the disguised maid they accosted in St James's Street, but supposing they did? What if they said something and caused embarrassment to her host and hostess? She had far too much time on her hands in which to imagine the worst, for Felicity was taken up with her friend and Lady Daneford was now the authority over their activities rather than herself. An added factor was the situation with Mr Garvey. She'd gathered that, like his friend Captain Stanhope, he had also resigned from the navy and would be taking up a position with one of the London hospitals shortly. He'd visited, without his friend , on several occasion and the object of his visits was clearly Felicity. What were his intentions and, in the absence of Baronet Fanshawe, should Cordelia have words with him? She suspected she ought to. This place had plenty of nooks and crannies to make use of and a couple could probably quite easily slip away from the ball. She quite liked the man, not least because he'd recognised her awkwardness when they encountered the two gentlemen in Bath and protected her by excluding her from the introductions.

At least Captain Stanhope would be present. It had been very wrong of Isabella to force below-stairs gossip out of her maid like that and more than once Cordelia had rebuked herself for not preventing it. But it was done now and the fact of his not returning to sea had become generally known amongst the Daneford household. A few days ago, at dinner, she'd heard Lord Daneford mention that an announcement had appeared in the *Gazette*, so now it was official.

More apposite, as far as the young ladies attending the ball were concerned, was the rumour, now apparently in general circulation, that the captain had not only resigned his commission, but was in line to inherit his father's viscountcy and the valuable estate that went with it. No doubt he would be much in demand at the ball and Cordelia doubted he'd have two words to say to her. Nevertheless, memories of his kindness to her came to mind, particularly the way he'd encouraged her to tackle her future when that crisis with Lady Millicent's illness threw everything up in the air. Somehow, he had encouraged her to break down the situation into manageable portions and take control of it.

That stimulated the thought that she might now apply the same methodology to her fears concerning the impending ball. She'd not long to go about it, for the ball was the very next day. It was the custom in this huge gothic monstrosity that was Daneford Court, for each member of the family to break their fast in their own chamber. Depending on where that chamber was situated, Cordelia thought it a sensible arrangement, for it could take such a long time to walk to the breakfast room that, as Lady Daneford had put it when explaining the arrangement to her daughter's young visitor, one might well faint with hunger along the way.

The usual housemaid delivered Cordelia's breakfast tray. Her room was at the back of the house on the second floor and there was a small table with two chairs positioned by the window, from where she could sit and enjoy a view of the formal garden below and, beyond it, an intricate looking maze of beech hedges and a backdrop of leafy woodland, in which were some welcome shady pathways, which she'd recently explored.

"Thank you Clara," she said, as the girl placed the tray of tea, toast and eggs on the table.

The girl curtsied and, as she quit the room, there was another tap and Serina appeared, with a garment of some kind over one arm.

"Good morning, my lady," she greeted Cordelia warmly. "I have found you a gown for tomorrow." She came directly over to the bed and spread it out for Cordelia to examine. "See, the underdress is of white satin and the light blue gauze on top will suit your eyes a treat."

"But…" Cordelia began, too taken up with how pretty the dress was to form the words. The overdress formed into points decorated with tassels, allowing the lace ornamenting the satin underskirt to show. But it was the top that was most unusual, for it crossed over the figure to fasten on the left side with more bows and tassels.

"Do not frown so, my lady, for it is my very own to lend you. I was also maid to the Lady Isabella's sister, the one before her. She left to get married and said she'd never wear this gown again, so gave it to me. As you can see I am rather too short and slight, not to mention old, to do it justice—besides, when would I have occasion to wear it—but I think it might be your size and should suit you admirably."

"It's lovely," Cordelia said. "Are you sure it won't cause objections?"

"I don't see why. Now, there are some blue kid shoes and white gloves to go with it. I shall find them now and return."

"This is so very kind of you," Cordelia said. "I shall feel like Cinderella!"

Left to her breakfast, for which she had suddenly developed quite an appetite, Cordelia felt far more cheerful. This lovely outfit must surely give her confidence. From there, it was a short step to considering how she might respond, were those two fellows to recognise her. I shall simply refer to the fancy dress masquerade tell them they missed a splendid occasion, she decided. Having supposedly missed dancing with her then, she might even dare to suggest they make up for it now! Finally, she determined to take Mr Garvey on one side when he arrived and ask him his intentions. Before that, she must also have a conference with Felicity.

Having experienced those high society events in London, Cordelia had assumed the ball at Daneford Court would be of similar proportions. Not a bit of it. Country balls in private houses were quite different. With a limited guest list it was a far more intimate occasion. Cordelia made the opportunity to visit Felicity in her room the night before the ball and it was she who informed her the party would number a mere fifty at the most and only half of those would be young people. Cordelia found the girl already in her night attire. For once she was alone, for Lady Daneford had insisted on an early night for her daughter and her young guest.

"All prepared for tomorrow?" Cordelia asked her.

The girl nodded. "Do you like my dress?"

Cordelia duly admired the pink crepe creation hanging ready for tomorrow. "The colour will suit you very well."

"And look at the sleeves," the girl pointed out—those slashes showing white satin beneath. They're the height of fashion."

"You'll look beautiful," Cordelia said, pleased to note the bodice's modest neckline, though refraining from making a comment about it, as she perched on the side of the bed. Neither did she enquire as to exactly how the girl had paid for it out of the paltry allowance from Baronet Fanshawe. She suspected Isabella might have helped.

"Felicity, I wanted to ask you about Mr Garvey. Has he...spoken with you?"

A flush rose up the girl's face, as she nodded. "I think he intends having a word with you, given the unavailability of my father."

"He's a good deal older than you."

"I know, but I don't mind that. I'd rather have someone...experienced, than the opposite. And he's a sensible man, as far as one can tell such things. He doesn't drink overmuch and he's not a gambler. It will be such a relief to escape from my father's excesses and be in charge of my own household. I know what people will think...because of the money. But he'd told me he's very fond of me. We even had a kiss during a walk in the woods. It was very pleasant."

"Well, I'll certainly speak with him, but I warn you that will include a strong suggestion that he must speak with your father as a matter of priority...and no more kisses, please."

"You're not cross?"

"No...but you must promise me to be careful."

She looked very happy as she smiled and nodded emphatically. "I know what's expected, Delia. I'm not as wild as my friend, you know."

Well, well, Cordelia thought, quite liking the way the girl had lately abbreviated her name in that way. It implied a growing friendship between them, in place of her more authoritarian role. Her job might well be done and she might soon be seeking a new position. What a relief to discover that her charge did, after all, have a mind and will of her own!

"Now about tomorrow," Cordelia added. "Shall I call for you and we'll go down together? Isabella will have to stand with her parents in the receiving line. You and I could wait together in the reception room for...a certain party to arrive."

"Yes, please," Felicity said. "I'm a little nervous."

So it went and Cordelia was pleased for both their sakes that the Stanhope party were amongst the first to arrive, for Felicity was on edge about her beloved seeing her in this gown. *I do hope he likes it*, she'd said, when Cordelia had met her to come down. On Cordelia's part, wearing this gown that fitted her so well it might have been made for her, came a self-consciousness that she'd never looked quite so grand. On passing Isabella and her parents, when the two of them entered the room, even Isabella had noticed her transformation, although she'd given no compliments. Rather, she had looked puzzled.

It was Mr Garvey who guided Captain Stanhope and his parents across the huge room to greet them and at once gallantly took Felicity's hand and brought it to his lips. "You look beautiful," he murmured. His companions duly curtsied and bowed and the viscountess then turned to Cordelia, who got the strong impression that no one had recognised her up to this point. She met the viscountess's eyes and smiled as she saw the woman's expression alter from polite enquiry as to who Felicity's companion was, to recognition. To give her credit, she recovered quite quickly.

"Lady Cordelia, how lovely to see you again, and what a delightful gown."

"Thank you, my lady," Cordelia responded, allowing her gaze to take in the viscount also, but avoiding meeting the captain's eye. What did he think?

Mr Garvey was now busy writing his name in various places on Felicity's dance card. Meanwhile the viscount was pointing out various other arrivals from amongst the county set they knew so well and took his wife's arm to wander about and greet them. That left her with Captain Stanhope and she nervously met his eye. He wore a gentle smile, friendly as ever, but broke the eye contact to bow and kiss her hand.

"Good evening, my lady. I have to say that, if your purpose this evening was to ensure our friends Farnham and Trumble fail to identify their favourite housemaid, then you have succeeded admirably. You look quite the part in that gown."

"Thank you. It's all down to the Lady Isabella's maid. She found it for me and even did this fancy thing with ribbons in my hair." She touched a hand to her head. "So I warn you, at midnight, I may well transform back into a maid."

He returned her smile. "In that case, may I reserve the opening dance and the supper dance too. I'm determined to see you eat a good supper. After all, scrubbing out hearths and so on is hard work."

Mr Garvey, who'd been having a quiet conversation with Felicity, now turned to Cordelia.

"My lady, perhaps you would honour me with the second two dances?"

"Of course," she said. He then stepped closer and whispered in her ear.

"Although might we sit out part of that time in order to have a little private conversation?"

She smiled, glanced at Felicity, and nodded.

There was no enquiring look or word from Captain Stanhope, which led Cordelia to assume that the captain was already in his friend's confidence.

Cordelia and Felicity had already met several of the young people attending the ball, for there had been a picnic at one of the other grand houses of the county, and Cordelia was pleased when Felicity took the lead on introducing Mr Garvey and Captain Stanhope.

"Come and meet some of the other young ladies," she said.

Cordelia watched her lead the two gentlemen from one group to another. She saw them dutifully write their names on various dance cards and felt an unexpected stab of jealousy that Captain Stanhope might well meet his future bride on this occasion. She'd overheard two of the maids discussing the fact that the future Viscount Stanhope was expected to wed and produce an heir or two as soon as possible, since his eldest brother had failed to do so.

The room was becoming quite crowded and Cordelia imagined that most guests had now arrived. That was proved when she saw the receiving party now leaving their post. Her stomach flipped as she realised that the awful Farnham and Trumble had just been announced and Isabella had stationed herself arm in arm between them and was coming her way. Surely not, she thought. She must mean to lead them to that group standing near her, to make introductions. But no, the taller of the two was staring directly at Cordelia and had bent to whisper something in Isabella's ear.

Cordelia drew in a slow breath, tried to stand a little taller and prepared to face them. *I shall not be a coward*, she vowed. The trio now stood before her.

"Cordelia, may I present Lord Farnham and Viscount Trumble. Gentlemen, this is the Lady Cordelia Penshurst."

Cordelia bobbed a curtsy, but kept her eyes on the two gentlemen. It was quite amusing to watch their expressions change from obvious interest in the girl in the blue gown, to astonishment and finally embarrassment. Trumble blinked rapidly and Farnham couldn't meet her eye. To have the upper hand in this situation was a delight.

"Oh, I believe we've met before, gentlemen, have we not?" She paused to enjoy the deeper hauteur spreading up each of their faces, before going on. "Was it not outside St George's Church some weeks ago, Isabella?"

Isabella clearly sensed the gentlemen's discomfort, but the fact that she could not account for it caused her some confusion. "Er…yes…I believe you are right," she finally managed to stutter.

Was it her imagination? She thought the two gentlemen actually looked grateful that she'd not exposed them. She'd make them squirm. Giving them her brightest smile, she continued.

"But surely, we met on another occasion, before that."

"I'm not sure, my lady," Farnham said, while his friend put a finger to his high shirt collar, to ease it.

Cordelia put a hand to her chin and gazed up, as if contemplating the possibilities, before looking them in the eye again. "I remember," she said, while the two of them appeared to hold their breath. "It was that awfully crowded masquerade at Willis's Rooms. I was somewhat differently garbed on that occasion and, naturally we all had on masks, but you stand out, Viscount Trumble, being so tall. I seem to remember we never managed a dance on that occasion."

Isabella now attempted to take charge. "Well, you are having the first with me, Lord Farnham," she said. Perhaps Viscount Trumble can do the same with you, Cordelia."

"I'm taken for the first two," she told them, "but you may have the third."

The men duly marked her card, Trumble for the third and Farnham for the fourth, although they looked less than enthusiastic about doing so.

Meanwhile, Isabella was studying Cordelia's dress and looking somewhat astonished.

"Surely, Cordelia, that is my sister's gown you have on. How did you come by it?"

Cordelia was ready, with her chin up and her best society accent. "Well, I don't know about your sister, but this came from a modiste in Bond Street. It was the height of fashion a year or two ago, but I can't do with constantly updating my wardrobe. What a good thing your sister isn't attending this evening. It would have looked odd both dressed alike."

Isabella knew when she was beaten. She gave Cordelia a suspicious look and led her gentlemen away. "Come and meet some other young ladies," she told them.

At that point, a bell sounded and chatter died away. The butler, who was acting as master of ceremonies, announced the start of the dancing. She joined the general throng moving through from the reception room to the substantial ballroom at the back of the house. Several long windows stood open to the terrace, which was lit with coloured lights, not unlike the Vauxhall Gardens. Cordelia had been a little nervous about being somewhat inadequate on the dance floor, but was delighted to find a fiddle-player warming up, with a man to call out the steps. It was to be country dancing. At that point a voice spoke in her ear.

"I'm hoping you know what to do, my lady. You're aware my own talents are restricted to the sailor's hornpipe."

Captain Stanhope was beside her and her middle fizzed with pleasure, as he took her hand and led her to one of the sets forming on the expansive ballroom floor. The opening dance was to be one where they stood opposite each other and did much whirling about and weaving, so there was really no opportunity for conversation

She wanted to say something witty in response to his joke about the sailor's hornpipe, but felt totally tongue-tied, caught up in all those feelings for this man which she'd tried to suppress. She only hoped it did not show on her face. She'd not seen him since quitting Stanhope Hall after breaking their journey there, since when his life had taken that unexpected direction. Glancing along the row of ladies either side of her, as they all waited to begin the dance, she once more wondered if his future wife was amongst them. At least she would have the memory of this evening in his company. That would have to suffice.

14: Repercussions

The Stanhope party was amongst the first to arrive at Daneford Court and Henry knew it was his mother's intention to be amongst the first to depart. While some guests, he was aware, had been invited to stay overnight, having travelled more of a distance, that did not apply to Stanhope Hall, which was a mere half-hour's carriage-ride away.

The welcoming party consisted of Lord and Lady Daneford and their youngest daughter. He could not miss the look Doc gave him as they walked across the entrance lobby to be announced by the butler. If Isabella's red dress at Vauxhall had been daring, this was…he could think of a number of adjectives to describe it…embarrassing was one of them. It was a deep-rose silk with quite a full skirt swirling from a tight waist. The bodice was covered in ivory lace and moulded closely to her figure, except the neck line must surely only just conceal her nipples. So much bosom was exposed that he suspected one bounce in a country dance would reveal all. Her shoulders were also bare, with the tiniest of sleeves made to cascade about her upper arms. As the girl turned to speak to her mother, he saw the back was even lower and the only thing holding the bodice in place was the laced ribbon up the back which ended in a tantalising bow at the top. He was astonished the mother had allowed it.

Greetings were exchanged, mercifully brief, since other guests were already lining up behind them. Doc had warned him about Isabella's change of affection and, sure enough, the girl saved her warmest greeting for him.

"Fie on you, Henry, for not visiting us with Mr Garvey here," she said. "You shall have to make it up to me by giving me the first two dances at least."

Henry said nothing, but simply smiled, gave a bow and moved on. "God spare me," he muttered to Doc.

"Ah, there is young Felicity," his mother said, indicating the far side of the room, "next to that rather beautiful young woman in the blue dress, the one with the tassels."

As they moved across to greet Felicity, Henry suddenly realised who it was who stood beside the girl. Did his mother not recognise Cordelia? Admittedly, it had taken him a moment, for he'd never seen her properly dressed up like this. She did indeed look beautiful and he was having some difficultly taking his eyes off her. She, on the other hand, while greeting his parents and Doc, seemed to be avoiding looking at him. His parents wandered off, while Doc was busy writing on Felicity's dance card, leaving him with Cordelia. At last she met his eye and he took her hand and greeted her properly. He wanted to tell her how beautiful she looked, but didn't want to embarrass her, so made a joke about not looking like a maid, which she responded to with a similar jest about being Cinderella. The ice was broken and he persuaded her to the first dance as well as the supper dance. Let Lady Isabella make of that what she would.

He duly claimed Cordelia for the opening dance, which frustratingly allowed no opportunity for conversation. He dearly wanted to ask her about the encounter he'd witnessed between her and Farnham and Trumble. Farnham, he noticed, was dancing the first with Isabella. From what he'd observed, the two gentlemen had been formally introduced by Lady Isabella and had immediately looked very embarrassed. A short while later he had observed both men writing on Cordelia's dance card!

As soon as the first set was over, Doc, who'd been dancing with Felicity, escorted her to join him and Cordelia. He was due to dance the second with Felicity and vice versa, but, having placed Felicity's hand in his, Doc promptly took Cordelia's arm. As if by prior agreement, the two of them then made their way onto the privacy of the terrace. Felicity quickly explained.

"Doc intends to…er…speak to Delia about his intentions…as regards me, that is."

"Oh, I see. Yes, he mentioned he had spoken to you. I wish you both joy."

"Thank you."

"You call her Delia?"

"And she calls me Flic. We've become friends, more than chaperone and ward really."

The next set was called to begin and they took their positions. He saw Viscount Trumble partnering Lady Isabella for this one. For his part, he had ensured he'd booked every dance with a young lady other than the determined Lady Isabella. Towards the end of the set, he spotted his friend re-enter the ballroom with Cordelia on his arm. Felicity saw them too, and Doc quite beamed across at her. The interview had evidently met his expectations.

The first half of the ball proceeded and he noted that he was not the only one who'd committed himself to every dance, for Cordelia also appeared fully occupied and more than once they briefly encountered one another in one of the hand-to-hand chains, or when one of them passed down the line in *Strip the Willow*. She certainly appeared to be enjoying herself. At last it was the dance before the supper break and he re-claimed her almost before her previous partner had bowed his thanks.

"Come," he said. "Let's get some fresh air on the terrace. I want to ask about those two ne'er-do-wells. You actually danced with them!"

Outside, Henry was aware of a few retreating shadows going towards the gardens below. Others were also taking the air, but evidently not confining themselves to the terrace. He led them over to the wall that edged the terrace and they both admired the pretty lighting around the paths of the formal garden. It was Cordelia who broke the silence.

"You asked me about Lord Farnham and Viscount Trumble," she said. "Yes, I actually invited them to mark my card, to make up for the fact that neither of them had managed to partner me at a certain masquerade ball, never mind that none of the three of us was actually there. They obviously thought *I* was. I had quite a surprise, in fact."

"How so?" he asked, aware he was so taken up with how beautiful she looked this evening, that he was not exactly paying much attention to her words.

"Each in turn did the same thing. I don't know if they'd agreed something beforehand, but it didn't seem like it."

She had his full attention now. "Just what did those blackguards do?"

"Oh nothing bad. It was quite sweet, in fact. First they apologised, which of course I graciously accepted, while suggesting a lower consumption of alcohol might be advisable. Then—which I'd never have anticipated in a month of Sunday—they proposed!"

"Proposed what?" he asked, puzzled.

"Why, marriage of course. They each asked for my hand. That is, they asked if they could court me."

Surely to God, she'd not accepted either of them, he thought. It could be a tempting proposition for one in her position. Neither was poor.

"You look shocked, Captain Stanhope. Why should it surprise you that someone might want to marry me?"

"I beg your pardon. Of course you are worthy of a proposal of marriage…but those two…"

"Worry not. I graciously refused them…the usual form of words. While sensible of the honour they did me, etcetera…"

What a relief! "I trust they were not too disappointed?"

"I doubt it. I think both were somewhat inebriated. I know Lady Daneford insisted on the fruit punch containing very little wine, but several young gentlemen, it is said, have brought their own supply of spirits."

"I think they need keeping an eye on. Some of the young women here tonight are very inexperienced and liable to…well, just to say I do not trust those two one iota."

"My main concern is that Flic is safe. I think she'll do very well with your friend. She's very keen to support his work and to make a practical contribution if she can, aside from…er…"

"The money." He finished the sentence for her.

"Quite."

Thinking of Doc quitting the navy naturally brought him to his own situation and he wondered how much Cordelia knew.

"Of course, I've resigned the navy as well," he said.

"So I understand. It will no doubt be a big adjustment for you."

"The ground not swaying under my feet, you mean. Yes, I have much to learn about the work of the estate, but my father is in good health and I anticipate many years before I have to take it over. Meanwhile, I have other plans."

She tipped her head, brows raised, by way of inviting more, so he told her of his parliamentary ambitions and his villa and small estate in Surrey.

"It may not happen for a year or two, depending on when I can get elected."

"I wish you the very best with it," she said. "I shall look out in the newspapers for accounts of your speeches."

"I can only express the hope that they are worth reporting," he rejoined. "What about yourself. It seems your role with Felicity will soon be done. What shall you do next?"

"I have no idea. I imagine something similar with another young woman. Once you get into this kind of work, apparently you can get recommended, although I doubt Baronet Fanshawe would furnish me with a reference since I've only seen the man once."

What a waste, he thought but could not say out loud. Suddenly, he had an overwhelming desire to kiss her, this sensible, modest, unassuming young woman. He wondered whether she'd ever been kissed before and somehow doubted it, for she'd been so young when betrothed to the Marquess of Dartington. Was she still waiting for him to return? All this was going through his head and he'd been unaware that Cordelia had spoken again.

"I do beg your pardon," he said. "I was lost in my thoughts."

"I only wondered whether you'd like to return to the ballroom?"

"Only if you would. I'm quite happy to stay here a while in peace and quiet and this pleasant cool air. We could take a walk in that pretty garden, if you like." He indicated the colourfully-lit walkways spread out below them.

"I'd like that."

Henry realised this was probably quite improper, since she had no chaperone. But it was still daylight and they would be within sight of the terrace, so he could not see the harm. They made for the far end of the terrace and he took her hand to steady her down the somewhat uneven stone steps, but at once let her go when they were on the path. He'd not been prepared for the wave of desire that overtook him, as he touched her, and tried to divert his mind onto practicalities.

"If we do a circuit, it will probably be about the right time to return for supper," he said.

"Nothing like a walk to build one's appetite," she said, as they proceeded slowly along the path around the periphery. "Do you get to your villa in Surrey very often?" she asked, clearly picking a safe topic of conversation, in preference to any further discussion of her two erstwhile admirers.

"Not as often as I'd like. I imagine we'll both be back in London for a certain event, not too long from now. I may take the opportunity to visit then. Meanwhile, it's in good hands. I employ a resident couple as housekeeper and caretaker. They're most reliable and very trustworthy." He thought of his rather valuable paintings, but did not mention them.

They'd reached the corner of the garden which bordered the maze to one side and a wicket gate leading into the woodland on the other. Henry had the wicked thought that he'd rather like to get lost in those shady woodland paths with this lovely woman. At that very moment, they both heard it, for Cordelia turned her head and looked at him in alarm. It was a woman's giggle. Someone was up to no good.

Cordelia pointed towards the maze. "It came from there, I think," she whispered. Should we intervene?"

"Assuming whoever she may be is in company with a man, then I think we must," he whispered back He stepped toward the gap in the beech hedge that marked the entrance to the maze. "Let me go first. Here, take my hand. It's quite dark."

It appeared the couple had not gone far for he made out the glow of a lamp on the other side of the hedge they were now walking beside. A turn to the right and then another and they were upon them. At once, Henry realised his mistake in allowing Cordelia to accompany him, for she was right beside him and could not fail to witness what was going on. Spreadeagled on the ground was a tangle of deep rose silk. Two stockinged legs with satin pumps on the feet protruded, while the girl's breasts were exposed—at least one was—the other was hidden beneath the back of a dark-haired male head. Trumble! He was sucking her nipple, while one of his hands was up her skirt between those ungainly-arranged legs and the other was opening the flap of his trousers. They were only just in time.

It was Cordelia's gasp that alerted the couple.

"What the devil!" Trumble shouted, while Isabella screeched.

Henry took the man's arm and pulled him up. "You're both coming with us. Delia, will you try and get her decent and then—my lady," he said, addressing Isabella, "—you will lead us to the kitchen entrance. I think it will be preferable to avoid your other guests witnessing your dishabille."

Once she had apparently overcome the shock of witnessing the pair about to undergo sexual congress—for Trumble's very erect penis had been clearly visible protruding from his trousers—Henry was impressed at Cordelia's cool manner. She was firm, yet gentle of tone, with Isabella.

"Come now, Bella," she urged. "You are quite all right. No one but us two have witnessed this. We shall borrow the housekeeper's chamber to tidy you up some more and then we shall discuss what is best to do."

In one hand Henry picked up the lamp the couple had brought with them, while the other held tightly onto Trumble's arm, in case he tried to bolt—though in all honesty where would he go? Once inside they found the housekeeper supervising the last of the trays of food being taken up to the guests. He watched Cordelia whisper something in the housekeeper's ear. The woman at once disappeared up the service stairs, he presumed to fetch the girl's parents. Meanwhile he placed the errant gentleman in the butler's pantry and stood guard at the door. "Wait here quietly, Trumble, and for God's sake don't touch that brandy. You've had enough. There are consequences to your actions this evening, as you know there must be."

When the parents came, Lord Daneford joined him and the miscreant in the butler's room, while Lady Daneford had the explanation of events from Cordelia. It struck Henry at once that Daneford was not at all surprised at his daughter's licentiousness. Had it perhaps happened before? Regardless of the answer to that question, on this occasion she'd been found out. The earl exited the room to have a word with his wife, before summoning Henry and the captive Trumble to the housekeepers' room, where Lord Daneford announced what would happen next in a voice that was firm and low and, thought Henry, cold with anger.

"Isabella…Viscount…you will both make yourselves presentable," he told them. "We shall then all repair together to the dining room, where your guests, Isabella, are currently at supper. Trumble, you will take her arm. You will both smile and try to look affectionate. I shall then announce your betrothal and there will be a toast. You will then spend the rest of the evening together and stay within sight of myself or Lady Daneford the entire time. Tomorrow, I shall visit the Bishop and obtain a special licence. You will be wed within the week."

Henry could not quite believe Isabella's reaction. She gave a whine of disappointment, which resembled a cat's howl and added, "Oh…but I wanted an earl, not a viscount."

He was even more astonished when, before either parent could react, Cordelia spoke. "In that case, Isabella, you should have been more circumspect about who you tumbled into the maze with!"

It reminded him of the time she'd joked about Trumble taking a tumble and from Lord Daneford drew a, "Quite so, my lady."

Henry thought Cordelia looked quite exhausted, so decided to take charge.

"Would you mind terribly if we didn't join you, Lord Daneford" he said. "We've managed to miss supper. I wonder if we could have a little something here."

"Of course," Lady Daneford said. "You'll find some of the leftover savouries have already come down. They're in the servants hall. Please help yourself and I'll send someone to make you some tea."

The Danefords and the happy couple departed, leaving them alone. Henry held open the door for Cordelia and they both took a seat at one end of the long table that normally served the needs of the numerous household staff.

"How are you, Delia?" he asked her and she looked up sharply. It was the second time he'd used the diminutive of her name and he liked the sound of it. It felt softer and less formal.

"A little shocked, I suppose, but in some ways hardly surprised."

Henry didn't say it out loud, but the thought did occur, that the Daneford couple might wonder just what he and Cordelia were doing so near the maze. What she said next told him she'd had the same thought.

"By the way, I told Lady Daneford that we were on the terrace taking some air when we heard giggling and went to investigate."

He nodded. "Very wise. I shall say the same, if asked. After all, one misbehaving couple is enough for one night, do you not think?"

She gave him a warm smile, showing those sweet dimples, and once more he felt that urge to kiss her. What was happening to him? For heaven's sake, surely he wasn't falling in love?

15: Return to Stanhope Hall

What a strange end to the evening, Cordelia thought. Never mind that she was supervising a young society girl and training her up for entry into society. It seemed she was receiving some instruction of her own at the same time. To witness the couple's activities in the maze was a revelation. So that was what happened when things went beyond kissing. Trumble had been about to, as the saying went, have his way with her. Thank goodness it had not been Felicity! On the other hand, Christopher Garvey was not Stephen Trumble. He was far more trustworthy.

She became aware of Captain Stanhope moving a tray of left-over sandwiches closer to them.

"I think we should both probably eat something," he said, "although they're getting a little dry at the edges."

She picked up the nearest sandwich and took a nibble. It rather cloyed in her mouth. "I'm not really hungry, but I really would like that tea."

"I'll chase it up," he said and left the room to find someone, leaving her to her thoughts. By the time he returned, bearing a tray, she'd decided what she must do.

He put down the tray between them. "They were still serving tea upstairs. I hope it's not become too cold."

Cordelia picked up a cup at once and downed it in one, never mind the temperature.

"That's better." She put down the cup and met his eye. "I've been thinking," she told him. "I don't want Felicity to stay another night under this roof and I suspect Mr Garvey might agree with me."

"I think he most definitely would. Let me consider a moment. He and I arrived with my parents, obviously, and the carriage is only a small one. Would you be able to get Lady Felicity's trunk and your own things packed and ready within the next hour?"

She nodded. "I don't see why not."

"Good. I shall confer with my parents, who I suspect are quite ready to go home now. I'll ask my father to have a quiet word with Lord Daneford to explain your and Flic's departure. They can take Doc and Felicity with them at the same time. Then I shall request they send the carriage back for the two of us and your trunks. I'm sorry that does rather leave you to do all the packing."

"I shall get some of the maids to help me."

"Good. I'll set things in motion now."

"But…are you sure your mother will be amenable to the invasion of two more guests?"

"She will be only too glad to help extricate you both from this embarrassing situation, I assure you. I'll find Doc and Flic and explain the plan. If you could take care of the luggage and be ready at the kitchen entrance within the hour."

Once he'd gone, Cordelia decided to eat a few sandwiches. Now that her exit plan had been devised, she found herself quite hungry. Then she set out to locate Serina and Clara, the two maids she knew and felt might be trusted not to gossip about the reasons for Felicity's sudden departure, although she had no doubt the entire Daneford household would soon learn the reason for the Lady Isabella's betrothal and marriage being accomplished in such record time.

She was reluctant to change out of her ball gown, but it was more comfortable to travel in one of her simple muslin dresses.

At last they were done and Serina sent Clara to summon two footmen to carry down the trunks, leaving her and |Cordelia to make a final check of both rooms.

"My lady," Serina said, "might I ask you something."

"Of course," Cordelia said, thinking it must be something about Isabella's behaviour and the reasons she and Felicity were departing so unexpectedly. However, it wasn't.

"I cannot stay and work for Isabella," she said. "Would you take me with you?"

"But…Serina, I can't afford to employ you. Besides, I don't really lead the kind of life that requires such personal attention."

"I don't care. I'll work for my bed and board."

"Well, I suppose…as a temporary measure. You could then apply for better paid work," Cordelia said, at once seeing the woman's eyes light up with hope. "All right…but you must speak with Lady Daneford first."

"I will. I'll meet you downstairs." With that she rushed from the room, wondering just what Lady Daneford would make of this. Cordelia suspected she would not be particularly surprised.

By the time the Stanhope carriage pulled up at the back entrance, Cordelia, Serina and the luggage were ready waiting. Captain Stanhope then appeared and at once assisted Cordelia up the step. He was clearly surprised to find Serina following and came to the wrong conclusion.

"Yes, after tonight's goings on, I think it a wise choice to employ a chaperone," he said, giving Cordelia a somewhat sardonic smile.

Was it Cordelia's imagination? Did he actually also look a little put out as he climbed in to join them and called for the driver to set off? She decided to put him right at once, not wanting him to believe she didn't trust him.

"Serina is leaving the Daneford employ," she said. "I trust that won't be too much of a problem and she can be found a bed tonight? Rather like us, she wanted to get away as soon as possible."

"I see," he said. "I'm sure that will be no trouble."

He gave Cordelia a look which was at once warm and resigned. It said he appreciated her trust. Did it also say he'd have preferred her company alone so they could talk? As it was they kept silence for much of the short journey. Back at Stanhope Hall, they found Mrs Rackham had waited up. She handed over Serina to another maid, and then personally conducted Cordelia to the very same room which she and Felicity had used to refresh themselves on that previous visit. How much had occurred since that day!

It was the early hours of Sunday morning when Cordelia finally got to bed. She enjoyed a wonderfully refreshing slumber, not stirring until her self-appointed personal maid brought her a morning tray.

"Good morning, my lady," she greeted Cordelia. "I've been asked to tell you the family will be gathering on the terrace for coffee at about eleven and would be pleased if you and the Lady Felicity would join them. It's a lovely morning out there. Shall I pull open the curtains?"

"Mm..yes…thank you, Serina. What's the time now?"

"Ten o'clock, my lady."

"I trust you were made comfortable last night."

"I was. The servants' quarters are very nice here. Should I lay out some clothes for you, my lady."

Enough was enough, thought Cordelia. "No, I'll manage. Perhaps you could see if Felicity needs any help."

How unexpectedly things had worked out, Cordelia thought, as she rested back on the bolster and sipped her tea. Had it not been for Isabella's misdemeanours, she and Felicity would still be at Daneford Court. Instead they were actually house guests at Stanhope Hall. She was under Henry Stanhope's roof as a social equal. What awaited her on the terrace? No doubt Lady Stanhope would be explaining the arrangements she'd made to get her and Felicity back to London sooner rather than later.

One of the maids delivered a jug of warm water and Cordelia rose and washed and dressed. This room was on a corner at the back and she discovered that one of the windows gave a partial view of the terrace. There was Felicity, already there and greeting the Stanhopes and, of course, her beloved Mr Garvey. She had better make haste and join them.

Mr Collins was in the lobby, when she descended, and he directed her through the morning room, where the French windows stood open, leading onto the paved terrace. The rest of the party were seated on elegant wrought iron chairs arranged around a marble-topped table and a maid was serving coffee from the tray that had just been delivered. On seeing her, all three gentleman rose and inclined their heads.

"Good morning, Lady Cordelia," Viscount Stanhope said. "I trust you are well rested."

Cordelia curtsied. "Very well indeed…and Felicity and I can't thank you and Lady Stanhope enough for providing us with sanctuary."

Everyone smiled at that.

"Indeed," Viscount Stanhope said, "and I know Lord Daneford is inordinately grateful for the way you and my son dealt with the situation and prevented the embarrassment that might have ensued. Now do have a seat, my lady, and enjoy some coffee."

The only vacant chair was between the viscount and his son. She'd still not met the captain's eye and avoided doing so now by looking across at Felicity, who was seated opposite her, between Mr Garvey and the viscountess.

"How are you this morning, Felicity?" she asked, as if she needed to! The girl was overflowing with happiness.

"Very well, thank you, Delia. Christopher and I have been discussing what is best to do, as regards my father's permission and taking things forward."

"Of course. I think we shall need to travel to London as soon as possible for that purpose."

Felicity glanced from Dr Garvey to the viscountess and then back at Cordelia.

"Well, actually," Felicity said, "Lady Stanhope has an idea."

The viscountess looked warmly at Felicity and then at Cordelia. "Indeed I have, my dears, I thought it would be much pleasanter for you both to remain here, while Mr Garvey travels to London to call upon Baronet Fanshawe. If you intend to arrange for banns to be read at St George's, it will be a month at least until the nuptials. Why not spend that time in the fresh air of the countryside. We have modistes enough in Bath to meet any need for special gowns and so on."

Cordelia frowned. "It's most kind of you, my lady, but I think I'm bound to speak with Baronet Fanshawe first…in preparation you might say. No doubt he will also wish to hear personally from his daughter's own lips…to verify the…er…engagement."

"There's no difficulty there," Viscount Stanhope said. "You can each write the man a letter. If we accomplish that in time to meet tomorrow's post, then Christopher here can spend a few days longer and time his arrival in Town for after the baronet has received his correspondence."

"Excellent. That's settled then," Lady Stanhope said. "We can all relax for a day or two and plan a visit to Bath sometime next week."

Cordelia did not demur, but there was a problem with this proposal. How on earth was Felicity to pay for expensive outfits from top dressmakers in Bath, when her father gave her such a token allowance?

The party on the terrace gradually diminished. Lord Stanhope went off to speak with the rector about some church matters that he'd not had time to discuss when he'd attended the early service. No one else had been to church apparently, so Cordelia wasn't the only heathen. Lady Stanhope excused herself to speak with the cook about dinner and the betrothed couple, now having only herself and Captain Stanhope as witnesses, decided it was in order to disappear into the gardens for a tete-a-tete, so leaving Cordelia alone with Captain Stanhope. She decided conversation might help, so began one, to try and take her mind off how close he was. She could smell that cologne she liked so much.

"Should we still address you as Captain Stanhope, now that you've left the navy…Captain Stanhope?" she asked him, unable to suppress a giggle as she did so and risking a quick sideways glance his way. He was smiling as he turned to face her and responded.

"I'm none too sure about that," he said. "I never enquired. Tell you what. Let us avoid the issue. You may call me Henry, or better still, Hal, which is how I'm usually referred to by my friends."

"Oh," she said, unable to keep the surprise out of her tone.

"No…rather…this is where you tell me in return to call you Delia...Delia."

She couldn't help it. She burst out laughing.

"That's better," he said. "After last night's events, a little levity is a helpful antidote."

His tone had lightened, but now he sounded serious once more.

"I must apologise for my mother. She does rather tend to enjoy taking charge. I hope you're agreeable to her suggestion about staying here until it's time to travel to Town for the happy event."

"It's most kind of her…of them. As long as it's not putting the household to too much trouble." She stood then. "Now I really must write that letter to Baronet Fanshawe. I believe I saw some headed stationery in my room."

"I'll leave you to it," he said. "Later, if there's time before dinner—which is at five I believe—I wondered if you'd care to have a riding lesson? We have a very docile pony who would suit you nicely."

Cordelia gasped and put a hand to her mouth. "I'd be petrified…"

"No…you'd be in very safe hands and on a leading rein, so you'd be going extremely slowly. Having found the courage to deal with last night's events so well, I hardly think sitting on a plodding pony would be beyond you. Come on. I know you're up to it."

The words he spoke were gentle and encouraging, but she read the challenge in his eyes. It occurred to her that this short period of a matter of two or three weeks represented a gift. It gave her the chance to spend time in this man's company. She might never get such an opportunity again, so she must treasure every word he spoke to her, every look and every chance to spend time in his company. That would furnish her with a precious store of memories to live off over the coming years of spinsterhood and loneliness.

"But I've nothing to wear," she said. "I'd rather not sit on one of those sideways saddles. Could I borrow some britches."

"You certainly may," he said, sounding pleased that she'd not made a further excuse. "I'll have them sent to your room. Meet me here at two."

Up in her room, Cordelia sat at the small desk, a blank sheet of paper before her. She'd never had to write such a missive before. It was vastly different to the light-hearted newsy letter she wrote weekly to Lady Dunwoody. Effectively she had to find a form of words that supported Mr Garvey's suit and recommended him as a future son-in-law. It was not unlike giving a character for employment. In the end she kept it as short as possible, but included the salient points—that he'd served on the *Europa* under Captain Stanhope for a number of years, had a fine medical career ahead of him and had the support of Viscount Stanhope. That last, she knew, would carry most weight.

At last the job was done and she was in the middle of soaking the wafer to seal it when Serina arrived with a shirt, jerkin and britches, plus some old leather riding boots.

"Tut, my lady," Serina said. "Everyone will think you a lad."

"I don't mind if they do," was Cordelia's repost. "My riding skills are non-existent, so I'd rather not be recognised."

Downstairs, Cordelia found Henry waiting as promised. In contrast to her makeshift costume, he looked very handsome, wearing a short riding jacket in a brown that matched his boots, and cream leather riding breeches.

"Ah, good," he greeted her. "Let's make for the stables and I'll introduce you to *Bluebell*."

Cordelia had never had much to do with horses. To her they were the dangerous creatures that went too fast when pulling carriages, something to be feared. The stable block was a short walk from the house on the opposite side to the chapel and she smelt it as they entered the yard, a combination of hay and dung, mostly the latter. Expecting to find the pony harnessed and ready in the yard she was surprised to find it empty. Henry sensed it.

"The staff has Sunday afternoons off, unless we need a carriage. Come…you can make friends with her first and then we'll saddle her up."

There were several horses poking their noses over their stall gates and whickering at their appearing, but he led them to one that seemed empty and opened the door.

"Oh, but she's so small," Cordelia exclaimed, at once visualising herself seated astride the creature. Her feet would be but a short distance above the ground!

"My father acquired her as a training pony for children. She's very docile and at ten years old quite used to novice riders. I'm sure you could manage something bigger, but a first ride on *Bluebell* will build your confidence. Come, stroke her nose, talk to her."

"Hello *Bluebell*," she said, tentatively reaching out a hand, which the pony responded to by stepping nearer and bunting her palm. It was not unlike petting large dog and she rubbed her ears and patted her neck.

Meanwhile, Henry fetched a saddle and bridle and soon had her ready. "We'll only be in the small paddock over there," he indicated. "Come on, old girl."

Once safely inside with the gate shut, he got Cordelia to mount, which was easy with the stirrups less than eighteen inches off the ground. He then let out the leading rein and told her to squeeze her knees to set the pony off. So they continued for about a half hour, plodding in slow circles. At last, Henry reeled in the lead.

"Enough for your first outing, I think," he said.

At that moment Cordelia heard the distant sound of carriage wheels and the jangle of harness. She looked towards the main drive. "Visitors?"

Henry turned to look too. "No one's expected," he said.

The carriage was now close enough to see the coat of arms on the side. It meant nothing to Cordelia, but one glance at Henry told her he recognised it. His glowering expression further informed her it was not a welcome sight.

"Come," he said crisply, "we had better get *Bluebell* back in her stall and repair at once to the house."

16: Unwelcome visitor

Sunday 12th July 1812

Henry was aware of how abruptly he must have come across to Cordelia as they ended the riding lesson and returned *Bluebell* to the stable. In turn she must also be aware that the reason had something to do with the carriage they'd both witnessed drawing up at the front steps of the house. Now he was striding in that direction, so fast that Cordelia was having trouble keeping up. He made himself slow his pace.

"I do beg your pardon, Delia," he said.

In keeping with his understanding of her nature, she asked nothing about the visitor or his own reaction to the arrival, but she did seek clarification.

"Obviously, I must get changed," she said. "Would it be best if I then kept to my room?"

"Not at all. On no account. I expect my mother has received…the visitor in the drawing room. Please join us there as soon as you can. If it is who I suspect, then dilution of her company is ever welcome."

It was too much to hope that a retired admiral had called upon them, with or without his lady companion. According to Doc, the old chap had planned an entire month in Bath to take the waters. Far more likely, unfortunately, was that he'd lent his naval carriage to the lady to return her to London and the wretched woman, having discovered the whereabouts of his family home, had decided to break her journey here.

He decided not to delay by getting changed, but make directly for the drawing room. After all, he'd not actually ridden, so his outfit was pristine enough. If it had picked up a hint of stable aroma, that was too bad. Whatever mischief she might be plotting must be nipped in the bud. He knew full well what she was capable of after that manipulative behaviour at Steven's Hotel. Provided Doc was present, he was confident his interests would be protected and the woman would not be able to hint at a relationship with her husband's former captain, as she had to the hotel clerk on that occasion.

They entered the house together, via the back entrance and Cordelia made for the servants' staircase, her most direct route to her chamber, while he went up into the lobby and thence to the drawing room, where he found Mr Collins at that moment emerging and closing the door.

"Well?" he asked the man.

"A lady calling herself Mrs Samuel Williams, sir. Claims to be a great friend of yours and Mr Garvey. Your mother has ordered tea."

"Who else is present?"

"Only the Lady Felicity. Your father and Mr Garvey have gone over to Far Side Farm. Their lad's broken his leg."

Damn, he thought. Doc was not here, nor likely to return for some time. He dreaded the tales the woman might have related to his mother!

"Thank you, Mr Collins," he said. "Lady Cordelia will be down directly. Please include her in the provision for tea and show her directly into the drawing room when she appears."

"Yes, sir."

With a slow intake of breath, Henry turned the knob and entered the room. Three female faces turned at once. On seeing it was him, his mother raised her brows in enquiry, while Felicity's features drooped in disappointment that he wasn't her beloved returned from setting a leg, and Mrs Williams...she had that gleam in her eyes and that sardonic turn to her lips...akin to the cat who'd got the cream.

He was determined that, short of throwing her out, he was going to be as rude as might be possible to the woman, within the bounds of convention.

"Good afternoon, mother," he said, "and Flic. I trust you and Doc enjoyed exploring the grounds."

"Oh, we did. It's so beautiful at this time of year."

He now turned to the visitor. "And I see we have a visitor." He gave a curt nod. "Mrs Williams...to what do we owe the pleasure?"

Out of the corner of his eye, he sensed shock in his mother's expression at his abrupt tone, but she said nothing.

Frances Williams' eyes narrowed as if she sensed he intended to do battle.

"Oh my dear Henry," she said. "There's no need to be so formal. I explained to your mother how solicitous you've been for my welfare since my loving Samuel died. How you came to visit me in Sussex and stayed a few days. Finding myself in this part of the world, I thought it only courtesy to return the visit. What a lovely home you have." She let her gaze roam the room until it finally came to rest on his mother. "You must long for grandchildren, my lady, to fill this delightful house with fun and laughter and secure the future."

That speech was the visitor's undoing, for it revealed her true colours to his mother and he saw understanding in her expression, which rapidly transmuted into a cool anger, for that comment had also touched a nerve that was yet raw.

"I am surprised to hear you speak so intimately to my son," she began. "He has never mentioned you. I know all his close friends and I noticed he addressed you as Mrs Williams. Has he in fact given you permission to address him by his given name?"

The woman put a hand to her mouth and gave what might have been a slight cough or perhaps an embarrassed half-laugh. "I do confess, such has been…Captain Stanhope's kindness to me, I may have misinterpreted his attentions in Sussex." She turned her focus on Henry then. "Please forgive me, captain. I must plead the distress of my bereavement on top of which is the further suffering caused by ignorance of the way my dear husband died. The navy tells me it was an accident, but I can get no other details out of them. Neither are they willing to pay me a pension, but they refuse to account for why I should be so deprived."

"That must be most distressing," his mother responded, sounding anything but sympathetic. "Are there no charities that can assist you?"

"That would be so humiliating. I had thought a kindly retired admiral might help me, but that came to nothing, except he lent me his carriage to get back to Town."

More likely, to get rid of you, Henry thought, but did not say out loud. At that point the door opened and Collins announced the arrival of tea borne on two trays by a footman and a maid.

The business of handing out plates and offering sandwiches and pouring the tea then followed, putting paid to further conversation for a while. At that point, Cordelia walked into the room. Henry had been alternately longing for her presence and dreading it. He did not particularly want her to meet Mrs Williams, but here she was. She'd changed into a cream muslin dress with an overall print of small blue flowers and she looked fresh and pretty. She'd evidently washed her hair as well and it was held back by combs, allowing a fetching arrangement of natural curls to tumble around her shoulders. The contrast between her natural beauty and the painted face and tight coiffure of Mrs Williams was marked.

His confusion as to whether he most wished to see Cordelia or not delayed his reaction and it was left to his mother to greet her, which she performed in a more formal manner than she might have employed, had Mrs Williams not been present.

"Lady Cordelia, do join us for tea," she said. "I trust you enjoyed your ride."

In keeping with the sensitivity he had grown used to witnessing, Cordelia at once got the point and replied in similar style. "I did indeed, Lady Stanhope, very much." She looked across at him then. "My instructor was most patient."

"Now, we have a visitor," his mother continued. "May I present Mrs Samuel Williams. Her late husband was once a Lieutenant on Henry's ship. Mrs Williams, this is the Lady Cordelia Penshurst."

"Delighted, I'm sure," Mrs Williams said, yet sounded anything but. "Penshurst, my lady? I don't recall…"

"My mother was Lady Celia Elderfold, Earl Elderfold's daughter," Cordelia told the woman, in an accent far more stately than that she normally employed.

"I don't recall seeing you presented. Surely we're of an age, are we not?"

"I was never presented, Mrs Williams, for I was already betrothed before I reached that age."

"Oh, that Penshurst," she said. "Now I understand. Surely it was not you I saw dressed as a boy on that little pony?" the woman then asked, presumably in an attempt to accuse her of unladylike behaviour on top of already having questioned her credentials for being on terms with a viscount's household.

The exchange, led by Mrs Williams, was so astonishingly rude that Henry and the other two ladies seemed to be frozen in utter disbelief, not least because it was done in the presence of the butler and two servants. He was about to intervene, but Cordelia voiced her response, managing to turn the whole thing into a light-hearted joke.

"Guilty, as charged," she said. "I judged it a sensible choice. The outfit enabled me to cling on tightly with both knees and, should that have failed, the size of the sweet little pony gave me less distance to fall."

She was delightful. They all smiled, although the guest's reaction was a little forced.

"Do you ride yourself, Mrs Williams," Cordelia then asked.

"I once learnt," she said, "but these days, I cannot afford…but enough of my troubles. I should really think of setting out soon."

Henry sensed the relief emanating from his mother, whom he would not have put past making some excuse and bringing the visit to an end herself, should that have proved necessary. He could not recall seeing her so incensed by a social situation before.

"Shall you travel through the night or break your journey?" his mother asked her, more he imagined to keep the focus on the woman's departure than out of any real interest.

"Oh, I'm in my driver's hands. I'm not sure."

His mother then brought things to a head by standing up and the rest of them had to do the same. "I'm sorry we cannot help in any way," she added. "As you've seen it's quite a small house and we're currently fully occupied." She turned to the butler. "Mr Collins, could you please see to Mrs Williams' carriage being brough to the front?"

"Milady," he said and at once departed, ushering the maid and footman with him.

Neither Henry, nor his mother, did the visitor the honour of escorting her to the front door. He could see that Cordelia, who'd missed the earlier part of the visit, looked a little surprised when Collins returned to lead the woman out and then shut the door. No one spoke until the sound of the front door being closed was heard, followed by the crunch of the carriage as it moved off.

"What a dreadful woman," his mother said. "Why on earth did you go and call upon her in Sussex, Henry?"

He shrugged. "I thought it the courteous thing to do, the man having once served on my ship. I remained a few days at a local inn to do some walking on the downs and I now very much regret accepting her brother's pressing invitation to dine with them each day. She clearly got the wrong impression."

"Why can't she get a pension?" Felicity asked him. "I do feel a little sorry for her."

"It's somewhat delicate and unfortunately no one in the navy is brave enough to tell her the truth." Henry told them "The man was once in my ship's company, but I requested he be posted elsewhere because he had a drink problem, constantly smuggling his own supply of liquor on board. He was a liability to the safety of the rest of the crew. The authorities put him to shore duties at Portsmouth but the drinking continued and I gather he fell from the wharf and was killed. It was judged his own fault, so no compensation and no pension. She's not friendless, but I think the brother is reluctant to offer her a permanent home."

"Meanwhile," his mother said, "she had thought to get her claws into you, Henry. I must say, I don't think I've ever been quite so rude to a visitor before. I doubt she'll ever return. I most certainly hope not."

Cordelia had not been present for the earlier exchanges so looked a little bemused, but said nothing, in keeping with her usual tact and restraint.

"I wonder how Doc is getting on with the boy's leg," Felicity said, clearly missing his company.

"I expect it will be the best mended leg the estate's ever known," his mother said, getting to her feet once more. "Now I must make my way below stairs to thank everyone for doing so well with tea, when they had no notice of a visitor."

Felicity stood too. "And I must finish my letter to Papa."

That left Henry with Cordelia. He met her eye and she returned his smile.

"We appear to be forever placed together in a room full of tea and sandwiches," he said. "Would you care for any more?"

"Mm…I think I would. Nothing like galloping over the hills to give one an appetite."

He picked up her cup and refilled it while she helped herself to sandwiches. "I'm wondering whether that is a mere euphemism for taking a pony ride, or some secret ambition of yours. If the latter, I'm sure we could build up your skills and achieve it."

"That might be a step too far, but I'd certainly enjoy another turn on *Bluebell.* She's so docile."

"Excellent. While this fine weather lasts, we can make it a daily outing."

She didn't reply to that, as she continued to nibble a sandwich between sips of tea. Then she met his eye again and he could see she had something to say. He tipped his head by way of enquiry.

"I'm probably speaking out of turn," she said, "but I did feel rather sorry for Mrs Williams. Don't you think she's entitled to be told the truth."

"Yes, I do," he replied at once. "However, it is not within my remit to tell her. The man was no longer under my command."

"It must have been quite difficult having someone like that in quite a senior position on board."

He nodded. "Extremely so. In the end I couldn't risk putting him in charge of a watch for fear of him taking the wrong action. Besides, the crew had lost all confidence in him. I tried to support the poor sod in taking control of the problem, but to no avail in the end." He just realised he'd used rather uncouth language in her presence. So relaxed was he in her company that he'd spoken as he would to Doc.

"It sounds a most frustrating situation. Shall you miss it, do you think…I mean the ship-board life?"

He did not answer immediately. It was a question he'd asked himself, more than once. "I'm not sure," he said at last. "Perhaps at first. It's a life of routine. I suppose I'll establish new routines. It's also a male environment. I could never imagine taking a wife on board with me, as some captains do. At some point, I shall no doubt get married. I think if I don't go about it soon, my mother is likely to arrange something for me! What about you, Delia? What shall you do once Flic and Doc are married?"

She gave a slight smile and raised her shoulders in a shrug. "Something will turn up, I'm sure."

"I'm sure it will."

They might have talked some more on such personal topics, but at that moment the door opened and Doc appeared.

"Hello! Am I too late for tea?" he said and his glance Henry's way conveyed his surprise to find him in a tete-a-tete with Cordelia, as he helped himself to a plate of sandwiches and took a seat.

"How's the boy's leg?" Cordelia asked him.

"A simple fracture of the tibia, which I've set. He'll be out of action for a few weeks, which is a nuisance for the harvest. I told the lad he must learn to knit and make a supply of good thick socks for the winter."

"I could go and give him lessons, if that would help," Cordelia offered.

"Excellent," Henry said. "It can be your incentive to progress your skills on horseback. We shall ride over there by the end of the week."

"The poor lad may never learn to knit in that case," she said, getting to her feet. "I'll leave you both to demolish the rest of tea. I must see how Felicity is getting on with her letter."

Once she'd gone, Doc spoke out loud what Henry had already seen in his expression.

"You're spending a good deal of time in company with Delia, my friend. Is there something we should know?"

"I…well, she's extremely good company. We laugh at the same things."

"More than that. She's personable, kind and sensitive, resourceful and, dare I mention it, would be rather nice to bed."

"My mother would never countenance it."

"Neither would she, I'm sure, at least not before the vows were spoken."

"Ha!"

"I take it the main obstacle is the footman?" Doc said.

"Partly. And no dowry, of course."

"Don't you see the way she looks at you, you dolt?"

Henry sighed. Did she care for him in that way? He must pay more attention. But what did it matter? Neither of his parents would contemplate such a match. It would set tongues wagging and potentially make the Stanhope name a laughing stock. Besides, she had this betrothal contract hanging over her and she was the sort who wouldn't want to go against the law. All told, there were too many things set against considering courting her. Perhaps he would be wise restrain his attentions towards her. But it was only for a week or two, until she left for London. He met Doc's eye again.

"You're simply a little love-sick, my friend. I know you said you weren't exactly seeking a love-match, but I've seen the way you look at her. You're each as smitten as the other. Anyone can see that."

"She's grown on me. Now, did I gather I missed a visit from the awful Mrs Williams? Did she have her old admiral in tow?"

So Henry told him about the unwelcome encounter, which kept them amused until it was time to go up and change for dinner, which had been put back to seven because of that lady's visit.

17: A wedding

Monday 3rd August 1812

Cordelia woke to the piping of a blackbird greeting the early morning outside her window. She and Flic, accompanied by the persistently loyal Serina had travelled from Wiltshire on Saturday by a privately hired coach arranged by Viscount Stanhope. She imagined Christopher Garvey would be negotiating the fee for this, as he had for Felicity's wedding gown, so she had not queried how it was to be settled. They arrived in good time to attend St George's yesterday morning and hear the third reading of the banns. In the afternoon, she'd managed to slip away on her own to call upon Lady Dunwoody and her talkative parrot. Although still an invalid, she was cheerful and full of congratulations for Cordelia's achievement in getting her ward a good match in her first season. "They did it for themselves, really," she told the old lady. "I had very little to do with it. In fact you probably had the greater role, having met him and Captain Stanhope at Westminster Bridge and made the connection!"

Now the day of the wedding had dawned at last, but there was plenty of time. She emerged from the covers and went over to check the clock on the mantel in the dim light. It was only half past five She made use of the necessary and got back into bed. She might doze some more.

But she found her mind was too active for sleep, not caught up in thoughts of the coming day. But of exactly what would happen once this day was over. One thing was certain. It was impossible to remain here in Baronet Fanshawe's house. The reason was not for any want of propriety, for the man was rarely present. Besides, she had the strong-willed Serina as both maid and chaperone these days. No, they must quit the place because it had been sold and the new owner was soon to take possession. As she'd told Henry, something would turn up. However, it did require some effort on her part to find that something and to be quite honest, she'd not found the time to do anything about it, for which neglect she really had little excuse.

True, there had been the wedding preparations, principally Flic's outfit, to see to, but Viscountess Stanhope had taken the lead on that, introducing Flic to her modiste in Bath to be measured, and then for the fitting. The kind lady had tried to insist she arrange a special dress for Cordelia as well, but Cordelia had equally firmly resisted. She knew Christopher Garvey, like Henry, had made a good deal of money over his years in the navy and would presumably be forking out for all expenses for Flic. From the day of his marriage, of course, he would be thirty thousand pounds better off.

"I don't really understand about these things," Flic had told her, "but Christopher has persuaded my father to move out of the big house in St James's Square in favour of a small rented apartment."

Cordelia in fact knew a good deal more about the arrangements than her young friend, for Henry had taken her into his confidence. "It was the only thing to do," he'd told her. "Doc discovered the house was mortgaged up to the hilt. There was really no option but to sell the place with most of the contents. He's set up his prospective father-in-law with an allowance that pays the rent on the apartment and gives him a modest income. It's all being handled by James Fagg and is so arranged that the man cannot change the arrangement without going through the lawyer. Somewhat humiliating for the baronet. I think he'd rather like to move into the new house Doc's purchased in Chelsea, but Doc is adamant that is not going to happen, not least because they may well eventually give over the principal rooms on the ground floor to running a medical practice."

That had been one of the few private conversations Cordelia had enjoyed with Henry over the remaining two weeks of her and Flic's stay at Stanhope Hall. The explanation for that would have been quite amusing, were it not so frustrating. In an ironic reversal of roles Flic appeared to have set herself up as Cordelia's chaperone. Suddenly she recalled her own youthful riding skills and longed to renew them. Thus, instead of trotting about the hills and dales of the estate in Henry's company alone, Flic, who turned out to be a very competent rider, accompanied them everywhere.

So it was that all three visited Far Side Farm with a supply of knitting yarn and some needles and the young lad with the broken leg had not one, but two tutors. He soon accomplished the basics and was put to multi-coloured winter scarves, since, as his mother pointed out, socks were a little beyond the novice knitter.

In all honesty, Cordelia knew the main reason she'd not put her mind to doing something practical to secure her future was that she had frittered away much of her time day-dreaming about those days she'd spent in Henry's company. As long as she'd been under his roof, dining at his table, socialising with his parents…she could conjure up the make-believe that there was some future in it. For his part, Henry was most proper in his behaviour towards her. Nothing he said or did gave the impression that his own mind might be imagining a growing affection between them, above the warm friendship that must be obvious to anyone who saw them together.

There had been one special moment, as fleeting as it was precious. Henry refrained from touching her, except this one time, which circumstances had necessitated. The usual trio had been riding and Cordelia had been persuaded to a different mount, more in keeping with her own height, but as docile and biddable as *Bluebell* had been. She'd managed the mounting with little difficulty, still wearing breeches as she was, and had enjoyed the sense of a more powerful animal under her. Back in the stable yard, the other two had dismounted already. Flic was leading her mount to the water trough. Henry met her eye.

"I don't think I can…" she began.

"Just try," Henry encouraged, standing beside her mount and holding the bridle. "Swing your leg over and hold tight to the edge of the saddle. I'm here if you overbalance."

She executed the manoeuvre too quickly and toppled sideways, at once finding herself caught in his arms. He carefully stood her on her feet, still holding her waist until she got her own balance. That was the moment their eyes met and she quite drowned in that blue gaze, unable to look away. She struggled to interpret his look. It was warm and friendly as ever, but something more, which she could not define, a depth, all the more striking for the seriousness of his expression. He was not smiling, but then neither was she. In the end it was he who looked away and let go his hold and the moment was gone. That is, it was gone in fact, but in her memory it persisted and she re-lived it most days.

Not for the first time, it crossed her mind that she would have been better to insist on bringing Flic back to London sooner and avoided all this heartache. How she could have justified such a move was hard to imagine. It certainly could not have been on the grounds of allowing

Flic to spend more time with her father, for it was racing season, during which period, they were all too well aware, he was never at home. Instead he spent his time up and down the country with as many friends and acquaintances as could tolerate his company, never far from the nearest race course.

The wedding service was to be at eleven this morning. There was plenty of time yet. Then came a tap on the door and Serena entered. It was early for Cordelia's breakfast tray. Then she looked again and realised there was no tray.

"Pardon me, my lady," Serena said. "You have a visitor. I explained you wouldn't yet have risen, but he insists he must see you…on a matter of some urgency, he claimed."

"Who is it?"

"Captain Stanhope, my lady."

"Oh!" She had to think quickly. Had something happened to Christopher Garvey? Perish the thought. Was the rector indisposed? "Where have you put him?"

"In the library, my lady."

"All right. I must quickly get dressed. Make him some tea and tell him I'll be down in ten minutes. Include a cup for me too. I'm not quite awake."

"Should I remain in the room with you, my lady?"

"No, Serena, that will not be necessary. I trust the captain utterly."

Fixed on the thought that his business must be something to do with Flic and Christopher and their wedding, she continued to contemplate what else might have gone wrong, as she quickly donned the same white muslin she'd worn for church yesterday. There was no time to brush her hair, so she fixed it back on top with some combs and let it tumble. He would have to take her as he found her.

She reached the foot of the stairs just as the kitchen maid was delivering the tray. She nodded her thanks and entered the room, closing the door once the maid had gone. Henry was on his feet, his back to the door, evidently staring out of the window onto the square. He turned to face her at once.

"Delia…I'm sorry to drag you from your sleep so early."

"I was already awake," she assured him. "What's this about? I've been imagining all kinds of obstacles to the day's events."

He stepped towards her and gently took her nearest arm. "Come, let's sit and have one of our perennial cups of tea. She sank into one of the armchairs in front of the fire place, while he did the honours and handed her a cup. She gratefully took a few sips and waited for him to begin. He took the chair opposite hers and sat forward. His brow was creased in a severe frown as he met her eye.

"Yesterday evening I called upon Lady Dunwoody to pay my respects. She told me you had visited earlier in the afternoon and spent a pleasant hour with her. But she was far from happy when I called, for, as she told me, there had been another caller between our two visits."

"Oh, dear. I'm sorry she was upset…but is that all. I was expecting you to tell me someone had died!"

"Hmm…not so much died as come back from the dead."

Cordelia knew at once. It could only be one man and it would certainly upset Lady Dunwoody. "The Marquis of Dartington!" she said. So it had come at last. Had that been him at the front door as she was leaving through the back? She'd heard the door-bell ring.

"He asked for you, but your uncle's butler was apparently very circumspect and simply told the man you no longer resided there. Then he asked for Lady Dunwoody and was told she was not receiving visitors. Given that your uncle also refused to receive the man, he had no choice but to leave."

Cordelia continued to sip her tea, recalling yesterday afternoon. When she'd left the house in Berkeley Square and walked the familiar route to St James's Square, there had been plenty of people about, couples out for a Sunday afternoon stroll, nannies with their young charges in the gardens. Quite probably one of the sole gentlemen who'd been ahead of her on the street had been him. What a narrow escape, although it was highly unlikely he would recognise her and vice versa.

"Delia?" Henry said, his voice full of concern. "Are you all right?"

"Not exactly," she said, aware of the tremble in her voice. "I knew this day might come, but now it has, I have to confess it's taken me a little by surprise. I'm astonished really…after all these years."

For a moment she watched him as he studied his hands clasped in front of him, his elbows resting on his thighs. Then he looked across at her. "Do you recall when I recommended you to use the services of James Fagg to help sort out your and Lady Dunwoody's situation?"

She nodded, for she had made use of his services for more than he knew.

"I think we must make him aware of this situation as soon as possible and see what he advises."

"Yes, if it becomes necessary. But, Henry, I've prepared for this day. I *am* prepared for it, I believe."

Henry nodded, but she knew he'd not understood her meaning. How could he when he had no idea what Mr Fagg had done for her?

"We need an urgent consultation with Mr Fagg," he said. When she did not at once respond, he added, "I apologise. I'm rather presuming here that you'd like my assistance with this situation."

"I…um…I'm most grateful for your concern, Henry, I really am, but this is a battle I must fight for myself. You were the very person who taught me that and gave me the confidence, remember? Mr Fagg has already been very helpful. Indeed, it is he who has furnished me with the weapons I require to contest the man's claims."

"He has? To contest the claims?"

She almost blurted out the whole of it there and then, but it had been Fagg himself who had counselled her against sharing what he'd found out with anyone, in case word got around and ultimately reached the man himself, so robbing them of the element of surprise, if he did appear back on the scene. Cordelia knew Henry saw her hesitation. In the end she decided this was not the time.

"I'll explain it all later," she said. "Right now I believe you are required to do your groomsman duties and I must see to the bride. I can't thank you enough for your support in this situation, Henry. I'm most grateful. I wonder…we don't want to spoil the day for Flic and Doc."

"Agreed. We'll say nothing, at least not until after it's all been sorted out satisfactorily, as I'm sure it will be." He stood, then. "I'd best be getting back to Steven's Hotel. I'll see you at St George's at eleven."

Cordelia got to her feet too and then he did the sweetest thing. He raised each of her hands to his lips in turn, his eyes never leaving hers. "Have courage. There is no way I will permit you to pay the penalty of your grandfather's misjudgement."

It was reassuring to hear him speak so, but she felt a rising determination to deal with the situation for herself. She would not hide away and let others fight her battles for her. But she *would* write a brief note to James Fagg to let him know the long-anticipated and unwelcome day of Dart's return had come round at last. His input might yet be needed. For now, she must concentrate on the immediate requirements of the day and not allow it to be overshadowed by the return of her so-called betrothed. That was all very well, but it was never far from her mind.

Amidst all the excitement of wedding preparations, no one noticed Cordelia's pensive mood, except for Serina. She knew something serious was afoot and that Henry must have brought word of it, but not the details and, despite the fact that Cordelia trusted the woman's integrity, she could not share the awful news with anyone.

So the morning got going, the household stirred, breakfast trays were delivered and Cordelia visited Flic in her chamber.

"How are you feeling?" Cordelia asked her.

"Excited! A little nervous. I'm so glad you're here with me. Serina said my father did actually return home last evening. I trust he'll be sober enough by now to accompany us to the church."

"I'm sure he will, Flic. He knows how important this day is for you. Try not to be too hard on him. I think he's probably quite lonely since your mother passed away and I imagine very unhappy. A man doesn't generally escape into the oblivion of drink or the beguiling pattern of continual risk taking for the thrill of a big win, unless he's lost any meaningful purpose in life. Perhaps when you and Doc produce grandchildren, he may find something to be joyful about."

"I do hope so." Flic rubbed her eyes and pushed herself into sitting position, seemingly focussing on Cordelia for the first time. "Goodness you're dressed already."

"Not in my wedding finery yet. There's rather a lot to do, starting with below stairs. The hired caterers should be arriving soon. I must go down and see that they know what they're about. Now, eat some breakfast Flic. You'll need plenty of energy for the day ahead. Serina will be here shortly to arrange your hair."

Cordelia's wedding outfit consisted of her best muslin gown, the cream one printed with blue flowers. With it she would wear a broad-brimmed straw hat trimmed with a matching blue satin band and a spray of small silk flowers and she still had those blue kid shoes and white gloves from the Daneford ball. How long ago that ignominious event seemed and yet it was less than a month since the misdemeanours that led to the quick, quiet ceremony, at which Isabella Daneford become Viscountess Trumble. There had been few guests, although Viscount Stanhope had attended out of loyalty to his old friend.

By contrast, Flic had warned her that St George's was likely to be quite overflowing for this morning's ceremony. The event had been notified in the newspapers and high society ever liked a wedding. The navy would also be well represented as well as various medical colleagues, especially from the hospital where Doc was due to begin his new appointment next month.

Cordelia supposed she ought to give Flic a little talk about what to expect on her wedding night, but quite honestly, she suspected Flic knew more than she did, at least in theory. She would simply have to trust that a man of Christopher Garvey's experience would treat his new wife gently.

There were clear gasps of admiration as Flic entered the nave on the arm of her father, who appeared sober, thankfully, and looked quite the gentleman in his formal black suit. Her gown was of ivory satin, quite simple, with the main ornamentation in the closely-fitted bust which was overlaid with lace. It took a surprisingly short time for the formalities that made her Mrs Christopher Garvey and the wedding party together with a limited number of invited guests were first to leave the building to make the short walk to St James's Square for the wedding breakfast.

Cordelia was grateful that Henry made sure he was beside her and took her arm.

"Holding up?" he whispered.

She gave him the hint of a smile and nodded. They'd reached the back of the nave and were about to leave the packed rows of seats behind them, when Cordelia became aware of a bearded gentleman to her right, who was staring directly at her. It was only for a moment, for Henry was between her and that side of the nave and soon blocked him from view. But in the few seconds she'd glimpsed the man she'd noted the bald head that contrasted so markedly with a greying beard and sideburns, the pale hazel eyes and the bony nose with a pink, shiny tip. It was him! Older now and portlier but surely, this was the Marquess of Dartington. He'd found her!

18: The elusive marquess returns

Before reaching Town to join Doc for his final few days of bachelordom, Henry had called at Banstead to check in with the Thompson couple and see all was well with his villa, for he was lending it to Flic and Doc for a brief honeymoon. Mr Thompson had vowed to re-instate the walled kitchen garden, so he'd also been keen to see the man's progress with the project. He'd driven himself in his own curricle and pair so as to have flexibility once he reached the capital, where he had business calls to make on his attorney as well as giving his love-sick friend some company and support.

Since quitting Wiltshire, he'd had leisure to recall the past two weeks, during which he'd spent time with Delia each day and observed her courage in conquering her fears sufficiently to learn to ride, even to the extent of trying a larger mount. Then there had been the occasions around the dinner table, when conversation had flowed easily and there had been laughter. He smiled as he recalled one evening, not long after that awkward visit by Mrs Williams and before Doc had departed for London. Doc, accompanied by Henry's father, had been to check up on the boy with the broken leg. It was his father who had begun the topic.

"Christopher tells me that he and I missed a visitor, when we were first on our medical mission a day or so ago."

"Would that we *all* had, my dear," his mother had said. "I doubt I have ever been quite so rude to a caller to our abode before."

"For my part," Henry had said, "it was a good thing I managed to refrain from speaking out loud the words in my head. They'd probably have been worse than even *Scarlet*'s colourful vocabulary." He'd smiled at Delia as he'd said it and she had smiled back.

"*Scarlet*?" his father had asked.

"Lady Dunwoody's parrot," Delia had explained. "I have a feeling he might well have been tutored by a rather uncouth sailor before Millicent acquired him." She'd glanced at Henry as she said it.

"Not guilty!" he'd said with a laugh as he held up both hands.

So the story of their early meetings and Lady Dunwoody's role in them, came out and he was aware of how, as he and Delia related it between them, both his parents had glanced from him to Delia with a quizzical expression. Yes, parents mine, he now said silently in his head, your reluctant candidate for marriage has indeed fallen in love. Too bad, it was with the wrong woman. He recalled particularly that moment in the stable yard when she'd overbalanced when trying to dismount and had fallen into his arms. They'd stood there, gazing at each other, unnoticed by young Felicity, who was leading her horse to the water trough. Had she not been present, he doubted much would have prevented him doing what he'd been longing to do for some time—to take Delia in his arms and kiss her passionately.

That period of daily contact with Cordelia had convinced him of two things. He most definitely had feelings for her that were a good deal more than simple friendship. But, while both his parents were courteous towards her, neither of them had said anything to him that would lead him to believe they supported a match there. Now he was in Town and the day of Flic and Doc's wedding had come round and he'd not seen Delia for five days. Had it got that bad, that he was now counting the days of not seeing her?

Fortuitously, as it turned out, he had visited Berkeley Square to pay his respects to Lady Dunwoody. It seemed the Elderfold butler had been busily employed answering the door that afternoon. Henry learned he'd only missed seeing Delia by an hour. Worryingly, however, there had been another caller and he came away concerned to make Delia aware as soon as possible that the infamous Dart was apparently back in England. The old lady was clearly fretting about the situation. Henry tried to reassure her that her former ward was not entirely friendless and he for one would do all in his power to prevent the marriage. "You must warn her he's back," Lady Dunwoody had urged. "She needs to know." He'd assured her he would do so as soon as possible.

His instinct had been to go directly to St James's Square for that purpose, but then he had second thoughts. Were he to call upon her that same evening, it was probable she'd sleep not a wink that night. He was not sure he would either, but common sense in the end prevailed. What benefit would derive from imparting the news immediately rather than waiting until the following morning? So he requested an early call from the hotel staff the next day and six o'clock found him at the Fanshawe house in St James's Square.

When he had finally broken the news this morning, he'd been somewhat surprised at how calmly she took it. Her reaction had been a strange mixture of surprise and resignation. Perhaps she'd been stealing herself against this occurrence over the years since the man's disappearance, so was half expecting it. But it was more than that. When he suggested consulting James Fagg, she told him it was not immediately necessary.

Meanwhile, he was reluctant to let her out of his sight. They agreed not to mention the awful news to anyone else and alone carried the tension of the situation. It was quite difficult for him and Delia to join in all the smiles and joy of the occasion with it weighing on their minds.

As predicted, the church was near to full for the service and it was a relief when it was over. The entire congregation stood for the wedding party to quit the church and make for the intimacy of a private wedding breakfast. Henry made sure he had Delia on his arm and a quick glance at her profile told him what stress she was under. They were almost out of the building when he felt her stiffen and heard her sharp intake of breath. A glance at her face told him she'd seen something in the pews to their right and he at once looked that way. A bearded stranger stood beside the aisle, but almost hidden from view beside him was an all too familiar figure—Frances Williams.

"Did you see her, too?" he whispered, as they followed Flic and Hal down the steps and turned towards St James's Square. "The woman's the limit. Are we ever to be rid of her?"

Delia stopped still for a moment and frowned at him. "Her? No, it was him. He was there! He saw me. I'm sure it was him—the Marquess of Dartington."

"Did he have a beard and a bald pate?"

She nodded and they began to walk on. Damn, he thought. The man was nothing but resourceful! Out loud, he said, "He must have been asking around and discovered your link to the Fanshawes and made sure he attended the service. I suspect his principal source may well have been Mrs Frances Williams. She was standing right beside him."

"Surely he can't inveigle his way into the wedding party?" Cordelia said.

"I'll speak with whoever's on the door, in case he attempts doing so," Henry said. "Try not to worry."

She did not reply and another glance at her profile surprised him, for she had a determined set to her jaw and he felt her step quicken slightly. When she spoke, her voice was low and firm. Gone was the shakiness of a moment before.

"I doubt I can avoid him forever," she said. "There's going to have to be a reckoning."

"That may be," he said, privately thinking he would do his utmost to prevent it. "Rest assured you will not be alone in dealing with the situation."

"Thank you," she said...and promptly changed the subject! "It's most kind of you to lend Flic and Doc your villa," she said. "It sounds like an idyllic spot and not too far to travel."

Henry played along, for what else could he do? "It's good to make use of the place. Heaven knows when I'll get to reside there. I believe their own house will be ready to move into by the end of the week." He couldn't exactly put his finger on it, but Henry had the feeling there was something she wasn't telling him in relation to the notorious Dart.

About thirty persons sat down for the wedding breakfast, including Doc's elderly mother, who'd managed the journey from Yorkshire. Toasts were given and speeches made. It was towards the end of the meal, when various guests were beginning to speak of going home, that Henry saw one of the hired footmen approach Delia and whisper something to her. She nodded and at once rose from her seat, excusing herself from Doc on her left and Henry's father on her right. She refrained from glancing across at him, seated between Flic and Doc's mother. What was going on? It could be to do with the domestic arrangements. Perhaps the hired caterers wished to begin clearing the table. But there was no sign of any of them hovering ready to do so.

At last, his curiosity and his concern led him to follow her out. How glad he was to have done so. He heard voices, male and female, coming from the entrance lobby and positioned himself out of sight at the end of the corridor that led from the dining room.

"You are quite wrong, my dear Lady Cordelia. I have every right to be here. I now own this house. I gave permission for Baronet Fanshawe to remain in residence until his daughter's wedding, but he is to move out before six o'clock this evening."

"I see," he heard Delia reply. "In that case, perhaps you would be so kind as to quit the premises until that hour. You are intruding on a private family occasion, sir."

"On one condition," the man said. "I insist on you accompanying me. I have gone to a good deal of trouble and expense to locate you and I am not having you slip out of my grasp now."

"Sir, I believe you are under the mistaken illusion that you have some claim on me. I should perhaps inform you that I have gone to considerable trouble and expense to prove the very opposite. I should also warn you that if you are fixed on pursuing these false claims of yours, there will be consequences, which you may not find very pleasant."

"Ridiculous girl! You cannot threaten me."

"No one should be threatened by the truth, sir. Now I suggest you leave, unless you wish the entire household to learn of your perfidy."

Good Lord, thought Henry. She was magnificent! He waited until he heard the front door crash shut and then stepped into the lobby. Delia heard his footsteps and turned. She looked quite white and her hands were clenched at her sides.

"You heard?" she said.

"I did."

"I'm glad. I've been wanting to tell you…" She tailed off.

"Come," he said, taking her hand. "Let's go somewhere more private.

So they ended up in the very same room in which they'd had their early morning conference, just nine hours ago, in the very same chairs, and Delia explained.

"When James Fagg guided me through our household finances and helped me devise a strategy, I also set him another task, which was to investigate the so-called Marquis of Dartington. He didn't take too long to give me some very useful information. He said it was fairly easy, using a publication called Debretts, for him to verify that no such title exists. There is a Hartington, but no Dartington. Having established that, he then checked the betrothal contract and various documents he had managed to acquire from my grandfather's suspect attorney, Mr Steadfast. Throughout, the name Marquess of Dartington was used and none other. Mr Fagg advised me that the legal conclusion in these circumstances is that the man has committed fraud, because he did not use his true name on legal documents."

"Are you saying the marriage betrothal is thus invalidated?"

She smiled and nodded her head. "Yes! And not only that. All the financial transactions were also fraudulent."

"And you've known all this time?" he said. Why had she not confided in him? She was not legally bound by any betrothal, but had not seen fit to share that knowledge with him. He felt a little hurt. But what difference would it have made?

She nodded.

"So you're free to marry where you wish." It was a statement rather than a question.

"Theoretically, but I doubt I shall."

On reflection, Henry mused, he had only himself to blame. After all, it was he who'd encouraged Delia to take control of her life and make her own decisions and it had furthermore been his advice to consult James Fagg, who had clearly done a lot more for his new client than sort out her finances! At his own recent appointment with the attorney, Henry had briefly referred to Delia and thanked the man for helping her. "It was my pleasure," the man had said. "It was gratifying to give such an intelligent lady the tools whereby to safeguard her own life."

That last phrase had not made much sense to Henry at the time, but it did now.

"Has the man admitted defeat, do you think?" Henry asked her.

"I doubt it very much. He's not yet been confronted with his fraud, nor the consequences that could ensue. Once Flic and Doc have departed for Surrey, I intend calling upon Lady Dunwoody, to apprise her of…recent events. The man's already tried to gain an audience with her. Should he succeed, I want her to be fully aware of the true situation."

"May I escort you?" He half expected her to decline, but to his relief she didn't.

"That would be most reassuring," she said. "I do occasionally tend to encounter difficulties in St James's Street."

He returned her smile at the memory. How remarkable that she could make a joke in her current circumstances!

The sound of chatter and laughter reached them. It seemed the married couple were making their departure. Henry opened the library door and he and Delia merged into the throng making for the front steps to see them off. Henry's father had lent his carriage and driver for the short journey to Banstead and they all waved off the happy pair. Soon the other guests departed, leaving Henry, his parents and Delia. He took his father on one side to request a word and they left the two women drinking tea in the drawing room. In the library, Henry poured them each a whisky and proceeded to recount the situation with the Marquess of Dartington and the fact that the obnoxious man was due to take possession of this house by the evening.

"Cordelia must come with us to The Clarendon," his father insisted. "I'll send a message at once for a room to be made ready. Before I do that, dear boy, may I ask what your own intentions are with regard to the young lady? Your mother and I are beginning to lose patience with you."

"What do you mean by that?" Henry asked.

"Well it's quite clear you're each very much in love with the other. Why do you think your mother insisted on Delia and her ward remaining at Stanhope Hall instead of coming to London. Have you still not proposed?"

"I thought you'd both object. Besides she's had this betrothal contract hanging over her."

"Nonsense. The girl can't help her mother's choice of marriage partner. We both like her very much. If this contract is illegal, there's nothing to prevent it. Stop prevaricating, before some other man snaps her up."

Henry downed the rest of his drink and got to his feet. "First, she and I have to call upon her former chaperone, Lady Millicent Dunwoody. We gather Dartington has been trying to speak with her and need to apprise her of the legal situation. Rest assured I very much intend to pay court to her, but not until all this business is behind us." He paused at the threshold. "And thank you. It is reassuring to have yours and my mother's blessing."

19: All is resolved

It had been a trial for Cordelia to get through the wedding breakfast after encountering the Marquess of Dartington in the congregation. The unexpected sight of him had quite removed her appetite and her face was aching with the effort of fixing a permanent smile on her face. At least Henry's warning early this morning had prepared her, just as James Fagg's investigations some weeks ago had fore-armed her for the battle that must inevitably ensue. And now it transpired that the man had actually bought the Fanshawe property in St James's Square! He must indeed have done well in business over the past eight years—with investments, she reminded herself, that actually belonged to her!

It was comforting to have Henry's support in all this and Cordelia could not fail to be aware, from his reaction when she revealed the outcome of Mr Fagg's investigations, that he was hurt by her not having shared the information sooner. She'd had good reason not to. How could a young woman inform a gentleman that she was not after all bound by a betrothal contract to another man without giving him the message, loud and clear, that she was available and open to other offers. No doubt she'd not have felt so self-conscious about it, had she not cared for Henry so much.

Now, once he'd finished the conference he was having with his father, Henry was to accompany her to what had recently become her uncle's home in Berkeley Square, where, between them, they would impart the news to Lady Millicent. Meanwhile Cordelia and Viscountess Stanhope were taking tea in the drawing room, while the caterers were clearing away the detritus of the meal from the dining room.

"Is everything all right, Cordelia?" Lady Stanhope asked her. "You seem a little distracted."

Cordelia put aside her cup and saucer, with a sigh. "I do beg your pardon, my lady. I'm not much company at present."

On consideration, Cordelia reasoned, there was no reason not to tell Lady Stanhope what was going on. No doubt it would soon become common knowledge amongst the *haut ton*, for had not Cordelia had quite openly sparred with the Marquess of Dartington in the lobby and no doubt several servants had heard their exchange, as well as Henry?

"A situation has arisen concerning my past, my lady." So she related the sorry tale and what she intended doing, with Henry's support.

"Lady Dunwoody resides with your uncle, I believe."

"She does," Cordelia confirmed.

"Might it be sensible to apprise him of the situation as well?"

"I doubt he'll receive me, my lady."

"But if Henry calls upon him, I think he'll have no choice. While you're about that business, it would be sensible to get your maid to pack your things. We'll arrange for them to be taken to our hotel at once. I think we should all be long-gone from this house before its new owner, whoever he really is, comes to take possession."

Cordelia already knew who he really was—another piece of information gleaned from James Fagg's investigations, which she'd failed to share with Henry. So it was arranged and Henry drove them the short distance in his curricle which he parked away from public view in the mews at the back. From there, Cordelia entered her uncle's house through the back entrance, as usual, and used the servants' stairs to visit Lady Dunwoody, leaving him to make his way around the building to present himself at the front door for an audience with her uncle.

Lady Millicent was, as ever, delighted to see her, as was her faithful maid Adèle, who at once went down to organise some tea.

"Now, dear girl," the old lady said, "I need to warn you about something…"

"Dart?" Cordelia queried. "You've already heard?"

"It's all round Town, my dear, as these things ever are."

"He's already tried to see you once, apparently," Cordelia told her, "but Uncle Harold turned him away. If he tries again and you feel up to it, I think we should see him together. He needs to be told a few home truths and if that doesn't succeed in driving him away, we'll have recourse to legal proceedings. Let me explain what my lawyer, Mr Fagg, discovered…"

Cordelia was completing her tale, when Adèle brought up a tea tray, set with four cups.

"Oo la la, so many visitors," she said, as Henry followed her into the room.

"Good afternoon, my lady," he greeted Lady Dunwoody with a bow.

"So much excitement! I've not had such an interesting day for weeks, dear boy."

"It's about to heat up even more, my lady," Henry told her. "That devil Dart is now below, along with that old family lawyer, the slippery Steadfast. They arrived while I was in conference with Lord and Lady Elderfold and Lord Elderfold had them conducted to the library, where he is now speaking with them. He will keep them in conference with him for as long as possible, but will then allow them up here. Let us prepare. I need to hide…perhaps behind the window curtain there. I shall only show myself if things get difficult."

Lady Millicent was clearly enjoying herself. "Adèle, go stand behind the dressing room door there. Then, if need be, you can run downstairs for assistance."

They all fell silent at the sound of footsteps approaching along the corridor. There was a tap on the door and Lady Millicent called, "Enter."

To Cordelia's surprise, it was not the butler, but Uncle Harold who entered. "Millicent, my dear, my apologies for disturbing you…and Cordelia." He nodded in her direction. "I have here two…gentlemen, who wish an audience with you. Are you willing to receive them? They say they are the Marquess of Dartington and a Mr Steadfast, neither of whom is known to me. If you receive them, I shall naturally remain in the room as chaperone."

Her uncle was full of surprised this afternoon, Cordelia thought, not only acknowledging her but now setting himself up as her protector.

Lady Millicent at once said, "Send them in."

They duly entered the room and Cordelia thought the Marquis quite uncouth, for he did not even greet Lady Millicent properly. Instead, he fixed his pale, somewhat close-together eyes upon her, just as he had in church, rather like a wolf focused on its prey.

"How fortuitous, to find my betrothed awaiting me." He stepped her way, seemingly intending to take her hand, but Cordelia side-stepped out of the way and held out both palms to dissuade him.

"Wait a moment, sir. I am not your betrothed and indeed, never have been."

"Stuff and nonsense. Steadfast here drew up the document. Lady Dunwoody was a witness."

The elderly attorney stood there, looking somewhat bemused by the situation, and nodded vigorously. "Quite right."

"Quite wrong," Cordelia said. "How did you sign yourself in that document, sir?" she asked him.

The man frowned and looked at the attorney. "Why, Marquess of Dartington, of course. That is the name I am known by."

"But it is not your true name. You were born Jack Benson."

"How did you…?" the man began, his face quite purple with rage.

Cordelia was merciless as she continued to unravel this man's identity. "It seems you were not aware that, for the purposes of effecting a marriage it is an offence to use any name but your true one. Your so-called betrothal contract is illegal."

The newly identified Mr Benson now turned to Steadfast. "What have you done Steadfast. You fool. You should have known."

"But, sir," the attorney responded in a shaky voice, "you never told me."

"Then we come to the matter of the money," Cordelia now continued, but before she could go on, Lady Millicent spoke.

"Cordelia, dear, I think *Scarlet* needs a little air. Could you kindly remove the cover?"

Cordelia wondered for a moment if Millicent's ill-health had affected her mind a little. Was she even concentrating on the exchanges between herself and Benson? Cordelia was about to confront him with financial fraud and Millicent was asking her to remove the parrot's cover! Nevertheless, to appease her, she did as asked. The bird immediately began dancing about on his perch, clearly happy to see the goings on he'd only heard thus far. Then the creature spoke and Cordelia was astonished.

"Steadfast has the money! Give it to Dart!" He repeated it twice more, in his sing-song cackle, until Benson, becoming more and more apoplectic, cried out.

"Cover the damn bird up, for God's sake!"

Lady Millicent nodded at Cordelia, who duly obliged, and then it was Lady Millicent who took up the cause.

"Witness for the prosecution, I believe. You see, gentlemen, I remember the private conferences you had in the drawing room downstairs. They were not quite as private as you thought. Scarlet's cage was there in those days."

"You have evidently been successful in your business in South America," Cordelia added, "but you began it with funds fraudulently obtained from my grandfather."

"What do you intend doing?" Benson asked her, less cocky now.

Before Cordelia could reply, her uncle joined in the conference for the first time.

"If you'd permit, niece," he said, "perhaps I could answer that. It is not so much a case of what we will do, but what actions you will take. First, you will place a notice in the main London papers announcing that you are in future to be known as Jack Benson. Following that, as soon as practicable, you will depart these shores and make your life elsewhere. Should you return, I shall personally see that you are prosecuted for fraudulently using up my niece's entire settlement and we shall seek redress through the courts.

Cordelia already knew that proposition was a fairly hopeless cause, given the lack of records, but Benson seemed to take it seriously.

"Damn you, Elderfold," he said. "Why couldn't you be a doddery old fool like your father?"

With that he marched to the door, crashed it open and strode out. Steadfast meekly followed behind, clearly not wanting to be left to the mercy of Uncle Harold, who—could she really believe it—appeared to have drawn Cordelia into the family fold.

It was he who now spoke. "You may emerge from hiding now, Stanhope," he said.

Henry pulled aside the curtain and stepped into .the room. "Thank you, my lord," he said, before looking at Cordelia. "Well done, Delia."

"And I believe we should also thank you, Lady Millicent," Cordelia said.

"And that mauvais parrot," Adèle added, as she stepped from her hiding place back into the room. Everyone laughed.

"He has a long memory," Henry said, "recalling a conversation from eight years ago."

"Ah…" Lady Millicent began. "In fact Adèle and I did a little tuition to help him remember. Useful, was it not?"

Everyone laughed.

"Is that tea still warm," Uncle Harold asked. "May I join you, Millicent? Adèle, if you would kindly fetch my wife? Stanhope, you're excused. I believe you have business with my niece."

What did her uncle mean?

"Yes, my lord," Henry said. "I'm to deliver her to the Clarendon Hotel. My carriage is parked in your mews."

"Excellent. I look forward to hearing of a favourable outcome in due course."

A strange way of speaking, Cordelia thought, for they'd surely achieved a favourable outcome already.

"Right," she said, "we'll leave you to your tea."

Henry tucked her arm in his and led her from the room. At the foot of the main stairs they encountered Aunt Florence, emerging from the drawing room. To Cordelia's utter surprise, far from snubbing her as she had not so long ago at Countess Cholmondely's conversazione, she was warm in her greeting.

"Ah, Cordelia, there you are, with your knight-in-shining-armour, I see. I'm to join my husband for tea with Lady Millicent, but I believe you're bound elsewhere. Mission successfully accomplished I take it, Captain Stanhope?"

"Indeed, my lady, principally by your very courageous niece, assisted by your husband and, would you believe, Lady Millicent's parrot. No doubt she will tell you all about it. For my part, coward that I am, I hid behind a curtain."

They all laughed and Florence had quite a gleam in her eye as she began to climb the stairs, but glanced back over her shoulder to deliver her parting words.

"No doubt we shall all gather together again when a certain happy event takes place."

Puzzled, Cordelia tried to consider what event this might be and whether it had anything to do with Uncle Harold's reference to a favourable outcome. Had she been paying so little attention that she'd somehow missed something significant in the conversation?

They passed down the service stairs to the kitchens and out to the mews.

"Goodness," Cordelia said, "where's your carriage?"

A quick check of the stables provided the answer.

"Ah," said Henry, "it appears your uncle's stable hand assumed we were to overnight here. The curricle's in the yard and my two horses look very comfortably settled in a large stall. Shall we walk instead? A short distance along Bruton Street will bring us to Bond Street and The Clarendon. It avoids St James's Street entirely."

"That sounds a sensible suggestion. You know how I prefer walking."

"Come then," he said, taking her arm once more to walk up the mews and turn onto Bruton Street. "In due course, I intend teaching you how to drive a carriage, now that you've built more confidence around horses."

"You do?" Cordelia said, quite bemused at hearing him suggest such a thing. On the other hand with his friend wed to her former ward, they would be bound to come across each other occasionally in society.

"Definitely," he said. "Ah, here's Bond Street." He brought them to a halt on the corner of the busy shopping street. "The Clarendon's on that corner there," he said, pointing it out. However, he did not move.

"Yes, I see it," she said.

"And there's that fashionable shop, from which you emerged to run into my arms." His glance switched from gazing along to street to meet her eye.

"And I seem to recall I was a little rude to you," she said, smiling up at him.

"A small price to pay for holding a lovely woman in my arms. That was more than two months ago. Do you think in that time that you might have revised your opinion a little in my favour, perhaps?"

"You know I have. You have been such a good friend, Henry. I would never have had the courage to tackle the awful Benson without your encouragement…and it was so helpful that you put me in touch with Mr Fagg. Is that the favourable outcome to which my uncle referred? I could not quite make sense of what he or my aunt said on our quitting the house—except it seems I am now in their favour. Is that something to do with you, too, Henry?"

The pavement was crowded with shoppers passing along in both directions, and Henry put an arm about her waist and guided her into a shop doorway, out of the stream of people.

"Possibly," he said, his gaze warm and his arm still holding her close. "I had quite a long conversation with them this afternoon, before joining you and Lady Millicent. It was naturally in part to acquaint them with the truth about your non-existent betrothal, but, as your senior living relative, I also sought your uncle's approval for what I'm about to ask you. I thought it fitting to bring you to the place we first met to do so."

Cordelia felt herself holding her breath, for it sounded as if he intended…surely not? She had thought it impossible he might return her feelings.

"Delia, dearest girl, you must surely know how much I have grown to care for you…to love you. I've so missed you these past few days and I long to be together, to share our lives. Dare I hope that my feelings are returned?"

Astonished, Cordelia put a hand to her mouth, before resting it on the collar of his jacket. "Oh Henry…Hal…I love you too, so very much…but I never imagined—"

Her words were stopped as his lips covered hers and his other arm came around her and he held her close, regardless of the two matrons who'd been examining the shop window and now, with appropriate gasps and tuts, moved on.

No sooner were the words spoken, than Cordelia began to doubt the possibility of finding happiness with this man. "But your parents?" she said.

"They adore you, Delia. They have been waiting to hear this news for some time—the news that is that we...oh dear, I'm not doing this very well. I'd not expected to propose to my future bride in such public circumstances...but here goes."

To Cordelia's astonishment he let go of her, bent down on one knee and took one of her hands in his. "My dearest Delia, will you do me the honour of making me the happiest of men by agreeing to become my wife?"

"Of course I will, dearest Hal." He kissed her hand and she could not stop smiling, quite overflowing with astonishment at what had just taken place, but with happiness too. Several passers-by had witnessed the event and a round of applause and congratulations broke out. They were both laughing as Hal stood up once more and then whispered in her ear.

"Might we find somewhere more private so I can kiss you properly?"

Arm in arm, they walked along to The Clarendon and Cordelia reviewed in her mind the events of the past half hour.

"Hal?"

"Yes, darling?"

"You deliberately arranged for my uncle's groomsman to stable your horses, didn't you?" So we would have to walk."

"That's a sorry beginning, if you believe me capable of such subterfuge. All I shall confess is that it was fortuitous *Scarlet* was not in the stables at the time I had my conversation with the groomsman."

"I knew it!" Cordelia exclaimed.

Hal responded with a smile, as they entered the hotel lobby and approached the desk.

"I believe you have a room reserved for Lady Cordelia Penshurst?" he said.

"Yes, sir...and would you be Captain Stanhope? Your room is ready also."

"Oh?"

Seeing Hal's puzzlement, the clerk added, "Lady Stanhope arranged it."

"I see. Well, I'll escort Lady Penshurst to her room and return shortly."

"Yes, sir. I'll have you shown up."

They followed the young assistant up the main staircase.

“I thought you were staying at Steven’s Hotel,” she whispered to Hal.

“Apparently not,” he replied. “I imagine you are beginning to realise how organising my mother can be. I sincerely hope you won’t change your mind!”

Cordelia reached for his hand. “Never!”

The lad led them along the first floor corridor and stopped by a door. “Your room, my lady,” he announced.

“Thank you,” Cordelia said, while Hal tipped him a coin. Perhaps now, in the privacy of her room, they might enjoy that kiss!” But it was not to be, for there was Serina standing immediately inside the door.

“I’ve unpacked for you, my lady,” she said.

“Thank you, Serina,” Cordelia said as she returned Hal’s somewhat resigned smile.

“I’ll see you later,” he told her.

20: Another wedding

Monday 10th August 1812

If anyone had told Henry, when he collided with an aristocratic young woman in Bond Street back in May, that she would become his wife in under three months' time, he'd have laughed them out of court. But here he was, on his wedding day, having stayed with Doc and Flic in their new Chelsea home last night. Hutch had managed to come south for the occasion this time, full of apologies at missing last week's ceremony owing to his grandfather's funeral.

Henry wondered how his parents were feeling this morning, particularly his mother. They had been delighted to learn of his betrothal to Delia, but Henry had put his foot down in regard to his mother's suggestion of a huge wedding in the estate church back in Wiltshire, which would have taken months to plan and organise. There were a number of reasons for refusing the suggestion, not all of which he felt necessary to spell out to his parents. He simply told them that he and Delia had discussed it and come to a joint decision that the arrangements they'd now put in place would work best for all concerned.

That conversation had been the only occasion on which he and Delia had been able to talk privately, a consequence of a strict regime of supervision instituted, he suspected, by his mother, who had enlisted the support of Flic and Serina between them to ensure the happy couple did not have the opportunity to anticipate their vows. Short of kissing her hand on greeting her each time they met, he'd not been allowed near her. They'd got away with more when on public display in Bond Street, for heaven's sake!

The conversation they did have took place during a walk in the park on the morning after their engagement, when at least Henry could tuck Delia's arm in his. The ever vigilant Serina followed them, ten paces or so behind. They both kept their voices low.

"Delia, my dearest, were we able to escape all this supervision, I would wrap you in my arms and kiss you senseless."

Their eyes met and she smiled. "I thought perhaps last night, with you staying at The Clarendon too, we might be able to meet up."

"Some hope, with me at the other end of the building on the third floor!" he said.

"And my prison-warder under strict orders from your dear Mama."

"There's only one thing for it," he said. "We shall have to speed things up."

"You mean not wait a whole month like Flic and Doc did?" she said. "That would be wonderful. But how would it be possible?"

"Well…let me see. One of my other elder brothers, Frank, is a bishop. I can obtain a special license from him. Hopefully, he'll bring it along personally and conduct the service for us. Where would you like us to get married, my sweetling? My mother has ideas of us all travelling back to Wiltshire and having a lot of county guests."

"Oh."

Henry could hear the reluctance in her tone. "I pointed out to her that such a long guest list would mean little to you or even to me, since none of them are on intimate terms with either of us."

"True," she agreed. "The most important people to be present for me would be Uncle Harold and Aunt Florence, now that we're reconciled. And of course, Lady Millicent, although I'm not certain she'd be capable of attending, wherever we hold the ceremony. Then obviously your parents and Flic and Doc and your other friend, Hutch."

"That gives me an idea," Henry said. "Why not hold it in your uncle's house? Lady Dunwoody could surely be carried down to the drawing room by a couple of strong footmen. The attendance would need to be limited to the number able to be accommodated in the drawing room. Some of your other uncles perhaps might attend. What about the Penshurst family, your father's people?"

"Sadly I've no idea. I never met anyone on that side. I suspect, from something I heard from the servants, that he got his education and training from one of those large orphanages, so I doubt there's anyone."

"If you're agreed, then have I your permission to take things forward. I can send an express to my brother today and then visit your uncle and aunt to arrange things with them."

She nodded. "When do you think…?"

"How about next Monday? Flic and Doc will have returned from Banstead by then and taken occupation of their own house. My parents are already in town, so only need to stay a few days longer. By the by, my mother wishes to get you a dress to wear for the occasion."

"That's most generous of her. As long as she understands I don't want anything too ostentatious."

"I shall tactfully issue strict instructions that your choice must prevail."

"Will they be very disappointed at a small gathering?"

"I think perhaps my mother misses having daughters. Now…shall we make another circuit of the pond? Do you think Serina's up to it? We've not discussed a honeymoon."

"A honeymoon? Where?"

"Immediately after the ceremony, what say you to a few days at my place in Banstead? Without your maid!"

"She seems to get on well with your mother. I was wondering if she'd care to employ her."

"An excellent suggestion. If you need any help with dressing or, particularly undressing, once we're wed, you need look no further than your devoted husband."

"You're very forward, Captain Stanhope. I'm not surprised your mother thinks you require strict supervision."

"After that, I had another idea. What do you say to a visit to Madeira? I have an open invitation from Godfrey and Dora to stay at their hotel."

"Oh, yes. It would be lovely to see them again and get some warm sunshine."

"Excellent. That's another fraternal epistle I must compose. We can explain all the arrangements to my parents this evening, at dinner."

They dined quite early and, to give them credit, even Henry's mother took the news of their plans quite well. It helped that Delia emphasised how important it was to her to have Lady Dunwoody present and, given that her disabilities prevented her from travelling anywhere, the only way was to take the ceremony to her. That argument won them over and after the meal, his mother invited Delia up to her room to view some fashion plates she'd had sent over by one of the neighbouring dress shops.

That left Henry in company with his father and they each ordered a brandy.

"She's lovely, Henry," his father said. "You're a very lucky man."

"Don't I know it."

"Your mother is a little disappointed at being deprived of planning a huge occasion, but I think she understands. The need to accommodate Lady Dunwoody won her over. That justifies the venue…but hardly the speed with which you are bringing this marriage about."

Henry met his father's sardonic eye and looked away for a moment.

"No…well…the fact is, were Mama not so fixed on keeping Delia and me apart until we speak our vows, we might have waited and had something bigger, perhaps a small ceremony at Elderfold's house followed by a much larger reception somewhere else. Then, of course, Delia might be with child by the time the wedding day came round, but who would know and quite honestly who would really care. Had Mama not determined that we should behave so properly, she might well have had her way."

His father's brows rose in what Henry assumed was amusement, but his words spoke rather of irony. "She and I anticipated things by several weeks. Godfrey was, as they say, an early baby. For God's sake, don't tell your mother I told you."

That had been but a few days ago and now the day had come. Henry was to ride with Doc from Chelsea to Berkeley Square, in his own curricle. Flic and Hutch had been collected by his father's carriage and the most important person in all the day's events was already at the house, being assisted to dress by his mother and Flic, no doubt with Serina and Adèle in attendance. The other important participant was his brother Frank, who had arrived yesterday in time to dine with them and meet Delia.

The bride and her entourage were naturally kept well out of sight when he arrived in Berkeley Square and he entered the drawing room in good time to greet the select group of guests before the ceremony was due to begin.

The sound of the double doors being opened quietened all conversation and the entire company turned to watch Delia enter on her uncle's arm. Henry couldn't take his eyes off her. She'd chosen a gown that suited her so well, a silvery-grey fine silk sarsnet over a white satin underdress. It had the modern high waist and the bodice had a regular pattern of small pearls sewn into it, with slightly puffed sleeves gathered into lace ruffles at the elbows. Their eyes met, hers, reflecting the colour of the gown, shone like silver. In a few steps she'd joined him to stand in front of Frank. The sleeves of Frank's white rochet outdid the modest fullness of Delia's dress and he wore a long black stole around his neck, making no concessions to his clerical garb, despite the secular setting for the service.

Henry had no idea what the form was, but he was damned if he was going to stand beside his bride without greeting her properly, so he turned to face her, gave a formal deep bow and then gathered one of her hands to his lips, pleased to note she wore no gloves. Then he leant forward and whispered in her ear. "You look beautiful, Delia, and I'm the luckiest man in the world."

Frank didn't seem to object, as he gazed benignly upon them, took up his prayer book and began the service.

How quickly it was done. The declaration was made and Henry claimed that kiss on the lips he'd been longing for every day this past week. With Delia on his arm, they circulated about the room receiving congratulations and good wishes from everyone there.

"Should we allow *Scarlet* a word?" Lady Dunwoody asked. "After all, he did have a helpful contribution to make."

"I suspect that might be singularly unwise, my lady," Henry said. "But you are welcome to expose him once Delia and I have departed. We shall leave you to your refreshments and whatever marital advice your feathered friend has to offer.

He and Delia had agreed to travel in their respective wedding outfits to save time before departure, although Delia added a lightweight cloak to wear on top against the dust of the road. Those who could do so came below to wave them off from the mews and Henry breathed a sigh of relief as they set off west for Putney Bridge and Surrey. They should reach Banstead within a couple of hours.

"How are feeling, Mrs Stanhope?" Henry asked, taking his eyes off the road for a moment to look at her. She certainly didn't appear on edge about being seated in a small carriage, but was quite glowing.

"Wonderful," she said. "Happy…delighted…it's astonishing to recall we were all attending Flic and Doc's wedding exactly one week ago and encountered that awful Benson man. I have to keep reminding myself it's not all some amazing dream. Tell me about your villa. I've wanted to ask about it, but we've not exactly been allowed much time together this past week. I know Flic thought it a lovely place and that Mr and Mrs Thompson were very kind and quite down to earth."

"Yes, it was a good find…all the benefits of the countryside but very convenient for Town. It stands in its own grounds of several acres, like a small parkland. There's a walled garden, good stable provision and a small paddock. By the gate there's a cottage, where the

Thompson couple reside. She'll be cooking for us while we're there. The house itself has three principle rooms on the ground floor and four bedrooms. Then there are the usual outbuildings for laundry, dairy and so on."

"Goodness," Delia said, "so large! I'd envisaged a neat little cottage on a small plot of land."

"I hope you'll like it," he said.

It wasn't long before they were turning in the gate and Delia's gasps of delight gave the answer. Thompson came to close the gates and greet them.

"Good day, captain…and my lady. The missus is in the kitchen doing you a chicken stew. I killed one of the birds this morning. Want me to see to the horses?"

"If you would, Thompson, thank you. Mrs Stanhope and I are hardly dressed for the part."

"And very fine you both look, if you don't mind me saying."

Henry took Delia's arm and led her to the front door, which was opened by Mrs Thompson.

"Ah, here you are," she said. "Now captain, you gotta do the business."

He had indeed, thought Henry, not for the first time finding both halves of the couple somewhat basic and direct. Delia was smiling.

"Good day to you Mrs Thompson," she said. "I suspect Captain Stanhope is not very practised in the duties of a new husband."

Mrs Thompson cackled with laughter, while Delia smiled broadly before whispering in his ear. "You're expected to carry me over the threshold, Hal."

"Ah…of course."

Scooping her up and indeed doing the business made him feel randy as a stag in rutting season and he was tempted to keep going right up the stairs and into the bedroom, but first they must do justice to Mrs Thompson's casserole. From the knowing look in Delia's eye as he set her back on her feet, her own thoughts were little different to his.

"Something smells good," Delia said, sniffing the aroma wafting into the hall from the kitchen.

"Aye. It's all laid ready for you. I knew you'd be hungry after your journey, then no doubt you'll be wanting to make an early night of it."

Henry managed to contain himself from whooping with laughter, as they took their places in the dining room and were duly served. At least the woman left them to eat without her presence, not that they did much talking, except with their eyes.

"Would you care for some tea, sir?" Mrs Thompson asked, when she came to clear the table.

They both smiled at that.

"Thank you Mrs Thompson," Delia responded. "We'll take a tray up with us. And thank you for the meal. It was very tasty."

At last they made their way upstairs.

"I seem to have left my maid behind, Captain Stanhope," Delia said, in her best hoity-toity tone, as they entered their room. "Might you offer some assistance?"

He didn't need asking twice.

THE END

Other period romances by Susan Leona Fisher

Regency Imposter series
#1 Doubtful Duchess

Classic Regency series
#1 Surprised by a Duke
#2 Tricked by a Duke
#3 Protected by a Duke

 # Regency Lady series
#1 His Haughty Lady
#2 His Capricious Lady
#3 His Philanthropic Lady

 # Regency Master series
#1 A Master of Speculation
#2 A Master of Industry
#3 A Master of Litigation *(short-listed for Romantic Novel Awards 2018)*

The Regency Secret series
#1 Her Secret Benefactor
#2 Her Secret Commission
#3 Her Secret Ambassador

The Regency Lady series
#1 His Haughty Lady
#2 His Capricious Lady
#3 His Philanthropic Lady

All available on Kindle, KindleUnlimited and in print from Amazon.com
(NB All are standalone stories and do not need to be read in order)

Author's website
www.SLFisherAuthor.co.uk

Printed in Great Britain
by Amazon

16341942R00103